re
L
v

Che
to
ww
wv

Love is
a time of enchantment:
in it all days are fair and all fields
green. Youth is blest by it,
old age made benign:
the eyes of love see
roses blooming in December,
and sunshine through rain. Verily
is the time of true-love
a time of enchantment — and
Oh! how eager is woman
to be bewitched!

EMMA DISPOSES

Charles Trevannion is annoyed by his recall from active service in the Peninsular on what he considers a wild goose chase. The chase leads him to a quiet Sussex inn and to a meeting with Nell Easton, who is apparently alone in the world save for a sinister-sounding uncle. Nell is able to help Charles in his task — until she herself falls into danger and stands in need of rescue.

MIRA STABLES

EMMA DISPOSES

Complete and Unabridged

ULVERSCROFT
Leicester

First published in Great Britain in 1972 by
Robert Hale Limited
London

First Large Print Edition
published 1996
by arrangement with
Robert Hale Limited
London

British Library CIP Data

Stables, Mira
Emma disposes.—Large print ed.—
Ulverscroft large print series: romance
1. English fiction—20th century
I. Title
823.9'14 [F]

ISBN 0–7089–3581–8

Published by
F. A. Thorpe (Publishing) Ltd.
Anstey, Leicestershire
Set by Words & Graphics Ltd.
Anstey, Leicestershire
Printed and bound in Great Britain by
T. J. Press (Padstow) Ltd., Padstow, Cornwall

This book is printed on acid-free paper

For Anne Walker

1

THE Colonel folded the sheaf of papers together with neat precision and laid them on the table. "If all these promises are fulfilled, we shall be almost up to strength again," he said thoughtfully.

"The new drafts have already landed and are on their way," said his companion. "The equipment was being disembarked when I left Bilbao. I pushed on ahead because I was anxious to complete my mission. But I can assure you that those lists are not empty promises. Men, stores and equipment are already ashore."

The colonel nodded his satisfaction. "It is very good of you to have taken so much trouble," he said with stiff courtesy, "and your news is all the more welcome because our losses in the recent fighting have been heavy." Over the past five years he had grown hardened to the steady disappearance of friends and comrades. One simply concentrated on

1

how best to fill the gaps left by death or wounds. After all, it might be one's own turn next.

The visitor allowed him a brief reverie. Then — "And the other matter?" he reminded gently.

The colonel's mouth tightened and his brows creased into a heavy frown.

"A preposterous suggestion," he snorted. "I'll have nothing to do with it. If he chooses to apply for furlough I must grant it of course, in view of your representations, but don't expect me to add my persuasions to yours."

His visitor was quite unperturbed. "In such a case it must certainly be the young man's own decision," he said gently, "but I think I shall find him quite amenable to my arguments."

The colonel's brows rose slightly, and a humorous quirk lifted one corner of his grim mouth. "Aye — do you so?" he queried. "You know him well, I take it?"

"I have never met Captain Trevannion himself, though naturally I am well acquainted with his uncle. But I believe that my case must command his willing service. You, I apprehend, do not share my opinion. And you must know him as well as any. Pray tell me about him."

The colonel shook his head. "I cannot claim to know him well. Not so well as Colonel Colborne for instance. It so happens that he had never come much in my way until I took over the regiment. And he is not an easy man to know. There is a reserve — a coolness. One is kept at a distance. But he's well enough liked in the Mess — and his men would follow him to Hell and back. In fact" — and his voice developed a snap that was barely courteous — "he's a damned good officer, and to be sending him off on a wild goose chase like this when any day may see us in action again is just the sort of stupidity that we've come to expect from those idiots at Horse Guards."

"I fear that they have shown little sympathy with your difficulties," said the civilian soothingly. "But I understand that Captain Trevannion is peculiarly well qualified to undertake this — er — wild goose chase. He is intimately acquainted with the district — it is his

3

calf country you see — so he would be the more apt to perceive anything unusual. Nor would his arrival cause comment — the so recent death of his grandfather would explain it. Obviously — a visit to arrange his affairs. While in view of the well-known proclivities of the late Sir Richard, a meeting with these smuggling fellows might well come about quite naturally."

"Yes, yes," interrupted the colonel, breaking impatiently across this mellifluous flow, "all quite true no doubt. But why now? What difference can it make at this stage, even if there *is* a leakage of information? We shall be over the Pyrenees before it can possibly affect the situation, and then" — he shrugged his powerful shoulders — "farewell Buonaparte."

"In military matters one can never be completely certain," said the civilian. "Last year, for instance," he waved his hands deprecatingly, "his Lordship cannot have wished to retire from Madrid. But let us not argue on that head," he went on hastily, seeing the colonel's deepening frown. "I can only

2

ENGLAND offered an indifferent welcome to her returning sons thought Charles, riding through relentless rain in the deepening dusk. First she choked you with the dust of the appalling roads, then she drenched you with an unseasonable July downpour that was fast turning the said roads into a quagmire. True that the pleasant green countryside and the homely rounded Downs were a delight to the eye after the arid plains and jagged peaks of Spain. But in Spain there were comrades and friends a-plenty to share the hardships and curse the weather, and there was work that he knew and enjoyed, work that he could do well. Here he was alone, save for Giles. He contemplated the immediate future with growing distaste. Trying to make bricks without straw, he thought. How could anyone deliberately choose such work? Lonely, chancey, dangerous. His thoughts turned for a moment to the dead boy whom he was expected to avenge. He too must have ridden these lonely lanes. Who, among the people he had trusted, had betrayed him to his death? How long had he lain a helpless prisoner, knowing what his ultimate fate must be? Such thoughts were not calculated to dispel the gloom that overlay his normally equable spirits. Resolutely he pushed them aside, and checked his weary horse, waiting for Giles to come up with him.

The one stipulation that he had made to Mr. Gressingham had been the admission of Giles into the scheme. Since the hobbledehoy of thirteen had first come to work in the stables at Trevannions, the two had been fast friends, cheerfully helping one another into various light-hearted pranks and out again. When Charles had gone off to join the army, Giles had been left behind, but the separation had been short-lived. At the end of his first furlough Giles had begged to go back with him. No, he had no fancy for army life himself. His brother had been army mad, and all he'd got out of it was the loss of a foot at Corunna. But surely the services of a reliable groom were indispensible, even to a young ensign in the 52nd Foot? Giles had had his way, and though he never ceased from grumbling at the impossibility of keeping horses in peak condition on army forage rations, he accepted all the other privations of a campaign with sublime indifference. In England the boyish friendship might have weakened and sunk into limbo. In Spain the years of shared tragedy and triumph had deepened and strengthened it.

Charles had insisted that he would not involve his old friend and ally in a maze that might well end in throat cutting unless he was permitted to warn him of the risks he would be running. Reluctantly, Mr. Gressingham had consented to a partial confidence. This indeed was all that was necessary. Giles cared nothing for the details. There might be danger — so obviously he must go along to haul his master out of trouble where necessary. As for keeping the matter secret — why — Giles was Sussex born and bred. Trust him to keep mum, and to present to the world a front of bovine stupidity that must baffle any suspicion. There was a comforting warmth in Charles' heart as his stolid supporter ranged alongside.

"We'll not reach Trevannions till well after dark with the roads in this state," he said, "and your poor brute has had enough already by the look of him." He eyed the jaded looking bay consideringly, for Giles rode over fifteen stone. "Better to rack up at an inn for the night and push on in the morning. We might try the Fleece at Wintringham."

Giles contemplated the suggestion with due care. The Fleece might promise shelter and comfort for man and beast. It was also the hostelry that had occasionally sheltered Gareth Penderby. To the Fleece his body had been carried by the fisherman who had made the shocking discovery. Nothing was known against the inn or its keeper. It might well be a perfectly respectable establishment, and in their present circumstances a claim upon its hospitality would be a natural proceeding. Yet Giles discovered in himself an instinctive aversion to that proceeding. Somewhere around the Fleece and its environs lay the secret that had brought Gareth Penderby to his death. Giles was no soldier. But he had rubbed shoulders far too long with the wily warriors of the 52nd not to have absorbed the basic principles of a tactical approach. You did not charge blindly into possible danger and ambush. He shook his head.

Charles waited patiently. Giles was slow to speech — but his ideas were generally worth waiting for.

"Better to sniff around a bit in Wintringham village afore we go busting into the Fleece," was his final conclusion. "Besides, it wouldn't seem natural like. Our Jasie keeps the Lamb, just this side of Springbourne. It's only to be expected that we'd go there, me only brother, and him a colour sergeant in the regiment before he lost his foot."

"Springbourne it is then, and the Lamb," accepted Charles. "Let's hope your brother can take us in. Maybe he'll be able to give us a pointer or two about the set-up in Wintringham. It's only a couple of miles away. He'd be bound to hear a deal of talk at the time of the murder."

"Well, Jasie was always one to see as far through a bush as the next man. I'd as lief as not harken to aught he has to say. And as for taking us in" — his face creased into a wide grin — "Emma'll see to that. A great one for the Light Bobs is Emma, having seen service herself in a manner of speaking. She was maid to Colonel Easton's lady afore she wedded Jasie. I fairly believe she'd turn out the Prince Regent himself to make room for anyone from the old regiment. Mind you, the Lamb's only an ale house, though cosy and clean if Emma's got aught to do with it. We'll lie snug enough there, I'll be bound," and quite exhausted by this burst of oratory he urged the weary bay into action and set off through the gathering murk in the general direction of Springbourne.

The lane which led to the village was eventually reached, but by then it was full dark and Giles was leading his horse.

"Go to bed early in these rural parts," remarked Charles, surveying the darkened cottages. "Let's hope they don't keep such early hours at the Lamb."

"There's maybe more going on behind

those window blinds than you might think for," retorted his henchman sourly. "Up to the neck in the smuggling, every man jack of them, and if so be as there's a run on tonight, t'would account for them all being safely abed. Leastways that's where they'll swear they was. Not a bad night for it, neither," he added, surveying the clouded heavens.

Nevertheless he was somewhat dismayed to find the Lamb, too, enveloped in the prevailing gloom. No welcoming lights shone from its usually hospitable portal. The windows were blank and unresponsive, and when Giles set the bell pealing furiously there was no sound of approaching footsteps. His jaw jutted obstinately.

"I'll take the nags round to the stables, Master Charles. Do you shelter here in the porch till I knock somebody up." He departed around the corner of the building, fulminating furiously on the habits of his errant brother.

Since he was wet through already, Charles could see little profit to be got from sheltering in the porch. He began to prowl along the rambling frontage of the inn, looking hopefully for some means of entry. He had the oddest feeling that he was being watched; that the inn, in spite of the blank face that it presented to the world, was quite definitely inhabited, indeed very much on the alert. Once he thought he caught a gleam of light reflected on to the wet cobblestones from an upstairs window, as though some heavy curtain had been briefly drawn aside to allow a hidden watcher to peer out. But his swift upward glance could detect no chink. Presently, however, he found what he was seeking. A casement window was standing slightly open. There was no need to force an entrance. He had only to release the catch and step over the low sill into the room. It was lit only by the glowing embers of a dying fire, but as his eyes became accustomed to the dim light he made out the shape of a lamp standing on a table near the hearth. He felt his way towards it, trying to avoid an array of heavy furniture which seemed to be largely composed of sharp corners and treacherously out-thrust arms and legs. A basket of logs standing convenient to the hearth suggested an easy means of re-kindling the lamp. With the skill of long practice he replenished the fire and sought amid the débris of the basket for a sliver of wood. It kindled easily, but the lamp proved more obstinate. A tentative shake indicated that it still held plenty of oil, but the wick was crusted. The splinter was burning away rapidly. Providently Charles blew it out while he searched for a knife to trim the calcined wick. The fire was beginning to burn up again and cast a light quite sufficient for the simple task, but the knife eluded him. Impatiently he thrust both hands into his pockets, and at the same moment became aware of a sudden draught which encouraged a sizzling log to shoot out a plume of smoke, and, almost simultaneously, of a human presence behind him. He turned quickly, half rising from his knees, but his movement came too late to avert catastrophe. Something struck him a stunning blow on the side of the head, and he collapsed in an inert heap on the floor.

3

IT was very queer. It must have been only a dream that he was back in England, for here he was, still in Spain. He could smell the smoke of the camp fires. But they were burning apple wood. Where on earth had they found that? Some poor devil of a peasant was going to find his orchard sadly depleted. He wondered how he had come to be wounded, and what had happened to Giles. The pain in his head made thinking difficult, and the effort required to open his eyes quite impossible of achievement. He lay still, trying hazily to assess his situation. He must have been carried off the battlefield, for he was certainly not lying on bare earth. And someone had put a blanket over him, a blanket that smelt, quite incongruously, of lavender. He sniffed again; quite definitely, lavender. Never a trace of wet mule or saddlery. It was very curious. Cautiously he explored his immediate surroundings with questing fingertips. He was lying, he discovered, in an extremely comfortable feather bed, and furthermore he was attired in a stiff and scrubby nightshirt that was certainly none of his own possessing.

At this point in his reflections he was disturbed by the sound of a stifled groan. Of course. He must have been seriously wounded and taken to hospital. It was an agreeable surprise to find it so comfortable. And having carried his careful reasoning to this point he relaxed for a little while, yielding to the clamour of his throbbing head. Next he began a careful process of flexing and stretching each limb in turn, in an attempt to discover the extent of his incapacity.

Very odd. So far as he could ascertain, he was perfectly whole and sound, apart from this blinding headache which still insisted that he would do very much better to lie perfectly still and keep his eyes closed. Submitting to this dictum, he lay drifting peacefully on the borders of sleep until the sound of voices disturbed him once more.

"No use arguefying, Miss Nell. You

know very well you'd no manner of right to go hitting the young fellow over the head like that, and him an officer in the old regiment."

"Well he shouldn't have come creeping through the window in such a stealthy fashion," retorted a second voice. A clear young voice this, slightly defensive and guilt stricken, but very determined. "How was I to know he was a soldier and a friend? It was too dark to see his uniform. I thought he was a housebreaker — or perhaps even my wicked uncle come to seek me out. He's very lucky that I only hit him. I might just as easily have shot him, but I thought the noise would disturb Emma."

This very reasonable explanation of her conduct seemed to satisfy the speaker, for she relapsed into silence. Charles lay still, trying to sort out the pieces of the puzzle. Emma. He was sure he had heard that name quite recently. Vaguely he knew that it had a comfortable sound. Now who was Emma? Cool fingers touched his wrist. A shade of anxiety had crept into the girl's voice when next she spoke.

"Isn't it time he was coming round? I

had not thought to have struck so hard. I meant only to render him unconscious so that I could tie him up."

"Giles said 'twas a new healed wound he had on him — and in course you had to pick the self-same spot to hit him. Wounded at the battle of Vittoria he was. Just to think — all through the Peninsula with scarce a scratch — for Giles did say 'twas just a sabre cut, though deepish — and then to be laid out by a female!"

On a soft gurgle of laughter, "Ah! But the female was British — and a soldier's daughter too," came the answer, and Charles, despite his headache, could appreciate the lilt in the voice which betrayed the speaker's smile. The mists which had dulled his brain were beginning to recede, and he listened with gathering interest as the girl's voice went on, "But I do wish he would recover his senses. He's horridly pale. Ought we to ask the doctor to see him when he's finished with Emma?"

"Now don't you go fretting yourself, Miss Nell. He'll do fine, though maybe he'll be a bit mazed like when he do come to himself. Stands to reason you can't really have hurt him — a slip of a lass like you."

"I did hit him pretty hard," she offered dubiously. "That was one of Papa's maxims. 'If you are going to hit, hit first and hit hard,' he was used to say."

"Yes, I daresay. And he was quite right. But they're not maxims for a young lady, Miss Nell, as Emma and me do be for ever telling you. Just see what trouble you've landed us all in! How we'll ever have the face to explain what happened, I just don't know. But I must be getting back to Emma. Sit you here and keep watch. If he wakes, he'll not be knowing where he is, and you can set his mind at ease, that he's with friends. And mighty queer friends he'll be thinking them," he ended, reverting to his earlier note of reproof, and Charles heard halting footsteps recede to the door, and the sound of its opening and closing.

Through lowered eyelids he was aware of a shadow passing between him and the lamplight, and presently identified a gentle rhythmic creaking sound as that of a rocking chair on polished boards. He did not yet feel ready for any attempt at conversation, so he continued to lie quietly with closed eyes. It seemed pretty obvious that the deep voiced man who had gone off to look for Emma was Giles's brother Jasie. Who the girl could be he had no idea, though from the terms in which he had addressed her she was probably very young — a schoolgirl even — and by her pure accent demonstrably a lady. A soldier's daughter she had said. And she had taken him for a housebreaker. The farrago of nonsense about a wicked uncle he dismissed as some private joke to which he did not hold the key. He wondered how long he had been unconscious, and what had become of Giles, and it was at this point in his musings that he once again felt the touch of the girl's hand as her slim fingers felt for his pulse. It was time, he decided, to stage his awakening. The child had meant him no harm, even if her conduct had been rash in the extreme. If it came to that, his own action in entering by the window had been foolish and ill-judged. It was unkind to leave her any longer in doubt over his recovery.

He debated for a moment how best to simulate returning consciousness, and in that moment the girl spoke, her voice soft but perfectly clear.

"I do wish you'd open your eyes. I want to see what colour they are." Almost, instinctively, he obeyed. Just in time the soft voice spoke again, and he realised that she was merely beguiling the tedium of her task by talking to herself, with no least notion that he could hear all she said.

"You've got nice hands," she told him, still in that same crooning undertone, and he felt his hand gently lifted and examined. "A soldier's hands," announced the voice, as its owner's fingers lightly smoothed the hardened skin of the palm. "And how long your fingers are! I think you must be tall. Of course I haven't seen you standing up. Oh dear! I do wish I hadn't hit you so hard, but truly it did seem best at the time."

Charles was beginning to feel slightly embarrassed. There was no telling how far the lady might carry her innocent commentary on his personal appearance.

He tried the effect of a deep sigh, and moved his head restlessly on the pillow. The voice did not cease its soothing murmur, but gentle fingers lightly touched his head.

"I expect your head aches dreadfully, and it's all my fault. I'll bathe it for you. That will make it feel better."

Now she sounded more like a mother tending a sick child, and less than ever did it seem possible to sit up and say, "Look here, I'm perfectly all right. Please don't make a fuss."

Meekly he submitted to having his forehead bathed with lavender water. The ministering angel was not particularly adept, and although her touch was gentle the cloth which she was using was overcharged with the cooling liquid. Charles, enduring manfully while trickles of wetness ran down behind his ears and soaked the pillow, had much ado to restrain his involuntary grin at the thought that the same small hand which had inflicted the injury should now be at such pains to soothe it. Presently the inevitable happened and the lavender water made its way under his closed lids. He bore with fortitude the stinging that it caused, but there was no stifling the shattering sneeze that the stinging precipitated. It quite convulsed him, and the resultant pain in his head was sufficient to render unnecessary a pretence of weakness. He was thankful enough to close his eyes once more and subside on to the damp pillow, while his attendant informed him rather haltingly that he was not to worry, that he was with friends, at the Lamb in Springbourne, and that he had met with a slight accident. Charles nobly refrained from opening his eyes at this polite euphemism. It was, in any case, less painful to keep them closed.

Having accepted this information in passive silence, he presently essayed what he hoped was a sufficiently feeble voice to ask for Giles.

"As soon as he and Jasie had got you to bed, he went off to see to the horses. They were near done up he said, especially the one he had been riding."

It seemed safe to display more obvious signs of recovery. Not without some natural curiosity to see the cause of his downfall, he opened his eyes. The lady was able at last to satisfy her ambition. Framed by the thick sooty lashes a pair of cool blue-grey orbs directed their steady gaze upon her. She found it oddly disconcerting. Not unfriendly, it yet held a measuring quality to which she was unaccustomed. She stiffened slightly, and her chin went up.

Charles, for his part, beheld a delectable vision, a sight to cheer the heart of a returning soldier long deprived of England, home and beauty. Seated in the low rocking chair it was difficult to gauge her height, but it was certainly not above medium. She was older than he had thought — definitely not a schoolgirl — her slim young body subtly but insistently feminine. A mass of silky hair, so dark as to appear almost black, was braided into a coronet round the proudly poised little head, and from this two or three soft ringlets curved casually to caress the whiteness of her throat. He paid scant heed to her other features, to the childish curve of soft lips or the beautiful modelling of brow and cheek and short straight nose. All his attention was for those incredible eyes. They were green. They really were green. Afterwards he was to realise that it was merely a trick of reflected light from the clear green of her dress, that actually they were of that changeable hazel that takes on colour from mood and background. Her complexion was clear and pale, but as he gazed it was suffused by a wave of soft colour.

Hastily he averted his eyes, guiltily aware that his behaviour in staring so was quite outrageous, and stumbled into apologetic speech.

"Forgive me if I seemed to stare. I had thought myself back in Spain — wounded, perhaps in hospital. When you spoke, and I opened my eyes to see a young English lady, I could scarce believe them and thought myself dreaming."

Nell's blush subsided, and her bearing relaxed. "Jasie said you might be a little dazed at first," she acknowledged. "Jasie is your Giles's brother you know, and the landlord of this inn."

"Surely — I think I remember — we found the inn deserted when we arrived? No one answered when Giles rang the bell, so I climbed through an open window while he was getting the horses into shelter. What happened after that? And why was the place in darkness? For it was not much past nine o'clock."

Not surprisingly the girl chose to ignore his first question and hurried into explanation of the other circumstances of his arrival.

"Jasie had gone for Dr. Hilsborough. And Bella had just slipped down the street to call Mistress Hannah. So Emma and I were by ourselves when you rang the bell. She said I mustn't answer it, so of course I didn't. One always has to do what Emma says. Even my Papa was a little afraid of her. She is a most redoubtable female."

"But why didn't she answer it herself?" demanded Charles. "Surely, if she's such an Amazon as you make out, she wasn't afraid to open the door after dark?"

"Oh no! But she couldn't." She hesitated for a moment, fumbled for a word, found it, and announced triumphantly, "She's — she's increasing you see. That was why Jasie went off for the doctor. He's dreadfully anxious because it's their first baby, and he's not accustomed to it."

This was said with such an air of grave feminine wisdom that Charles badly wanted to laugh, and put up a hand to hide the smile that would certainly give offence to so young a damsel. The action was misconstrued.

"There now — you've made your headache worse with talking too much," she scolded, rising quickly from her chair. "Would you like me to bathe your head again?"

Charles declined this offer with rather more haste than courtesy, whereupon she announced her intention of getting Dr. Hilsborough to mix him a soothing draught before he left the house. "Then you will feel very much more the thing," she promised him confidently.

Fortunately, before there was time to implement this helpful notion the bedroom door creaked open and Giles's tousled head appeared round it. Seeing his master's eyes open, his face creased into a relieved grin and he advanced boldly to the bedside. His first words however were addressed to the lady.

"Jasie says I'm to tell you all's well and

it's a boy. And Mistress Hannah says you can go along and see Emma for a minute if you've a mind to."

The girl looked pleased and nodded acquiescence. "There! I told Jasie it would be so, and no need to fret. He might know he could depend on Emma. Where's the doctor? I hope he hasn't gone off. I want him to mix a composer for Captain Trevannion."

Giles looked mildly surprised, but said that the doctor had only gone down to the parlour, where Jasie was doubtless seeing to his refreshment.

"Then I'll run down and see him straight away before I go to Emma," exclaimed the girl impetuously, and was gone from the room before Charles could express his opinion of soothing draughts. Nor could he suborn Giles to his assistance. The big groom declared that he was well served for running head on into an embuscade as soon as he was left to his own devices.

"And who's the girl, and what is she doing running loose in an ale house?" demanded Charles, when Giles had finally come to the end of his comments on his master's folly.

Giles grinned. "That, sir, is Miss Helen Easton. And she'll run loose anywhere, for she's never been broke to bridle."

"Easton?" said Charles, on a startled note. "Related to Colonel Easton of ours?"

"Aye — poor little lass," nodded Giles. "His only child. And an orphan since Badajos, for seemingly her mother died only a few months before."

"But what's she doing here? Surely she must have relatives who could give her a home?"

Giles shrugged. "As to that I'd not be knowing. Jasie didn't say much about her. Too took up with Emma and his son. But I recognised the little wench straight off. She and her mother were with the regiment at Shorncliffe. I wonder you don't remember her, for a proper madcap she was, and crazy about the horses. Always slipping off to the stables whenever she could escape from her governess. Her mother was a sweet gentle lady, but sickly. Her papa was the only one Miss Helen minded, and he backed her up in most of her mischief. Brought her up more like a lad than a little lady. Military discipline he said was the way to control her, and he taught her to fence and shoot and ride and never to fear a tumble. I did hear tell she was a fair shot — for a female of course."

Charles laughed, in spite of the pain it gave him. "In that case I must be thankful, as the lady herself said, that she decided not to shoot me but only to break my head. At the time I thought she was romancing."

Giles cocked an enquiring eyebrow.

"She was talking to your brother who was trying, without much success, to convince her of the impropriety of her behaviour. Apparently she only decided against shooting because the noise might disturb Emma. I must certainly remember to express my gratitude to your sister-in-law."

"Aye, she's a proper little varmint is Miss Helen," agreed Giles, "but she was as sorry as anything when I explained who you were, and nothing would do for her but to look after you herself while I saw to the nags. Which we were main glad of, with the house in such an uproar over this young nevvy of mine."

"Well let her go nurse your nephew but keep her out of here," retorted Charles. "All I need is a night's sleep to set me to rights. Do you go and see if you can fend off this doctor and his draught. A composer indeed!"

Giles rubbed his nose reflectively. "Might serve us a good turn, Master Charles. You could make out to be worse than you are. Give us an excuse to stop on here a day or two, and it's a deal more handy for our job than Trevannions."

Charles mulled the suggestion over. "You're right of course," he agreed, "but we can scarcely expect your brother to put us up under the circumstances. With his wife laid up he'll have enough on his hands."

"Oh no, sir! He's got plenty of help in the house. Jasie wouldn't go for to turn you out — a badly injured man!" declared Giles soulfully.

"Any more of your impudence, my lad, and there'll *be* a badly injured man," grunted Charles. "And a fine fool I'm going to look, lying here moaning about a knock on the head. But you're right as usual, damn you. Lead on your doctor. But I'm hanged if I'm swallowing his poisonous potion. You can get rid of *that* for me, even if it comes to swallowing it yourself. And keep Miss Easton and her lavender water out of here," he concluded, turning over his damp pillow and arranging himself to portray the picture of a man in the last extreme of exhaustion and pain.

4

HE woke early with a pleasant feeling of well-being. Sunshine was playing gently over the bed from the open casement. The air was pleasantly fresh after yesterday's rain, and sweet with the scent of the honeysuckle that wreathed the window frame. He had slept soundly and long without benefit of Dr. Hilsborough's draught. Giles had obediently disposed of that, supplying instead a generous platter of beef sandwiches and a tankard of his brother's home brewed, which he smuggled in to the 'invalid' after the rest of the household had finally gone to bed.

Thus fortified, Charles had promptly gone to sleep, and now felt none the worse for his misadventure of the previous evening. It was going to be difficult to play the invalid convincingly. Already he was remarkably hungry, and the tantalising odours of coffee and frying ham which presently drifted through the window to mingle with the heavy sweetness of the honeysuckle did nothing to diminish his appetite. With growing impatience he awaited the arrival of Giles. But the knock which eventually sounded on the door panel heralded the arrival of Miss Helen Easton, carrying a coffee pot and attended by a sturdy looking damsel bearing a well laden tray.

"Oh! You look so much better this morning," she cried. "Dr. Hilsborough will be much relieved. He was quite anxious about you last night, fearing some hidden injury, since he could find nothing to account for the symptoms that you described. I shall tell him that his draught has quite restored you. The improvement is almost magical."

Entirely magical, agreed Charles, whole-heartedly if silently, remembering how Giles had poured the evil looking concoction out of the window, where doubtless it was applying its beneficial properties to the roots of the honeysuckle.

Miss Easton directed the maid to draw up a stool which would accommodate the coffee pot and arranged the tray to her satisfaction, explaining the while that Giles was busy in the stable but would be up to wait on his master before very long. "He would have brought up your breakfast, but I wished to bring it myself so that I could speak to you. Yes, that will do nicely, Bella. You can go down now and help Mistress Hannah. I shall not be very long."

Charles eyed Miss Easton with some misgivings. He wished she would go away and allow him to enjoy his breakfast in peace. She was standing very straight beside the bed, her hands tightly clasped at her breast, and he suddenly realised that she was desperately nervous.

"Yes?" he said on a note of encouragement, for the ham was going cold.

"I told you a lie yesterday," she brought out breathlessly. "I said you'd met with an accident. You didn't. I hit you, because I thought you were a housebreaker."

Her head was well up, but Charles could see that her lips were quivering and a little pulse in her throat was beating furiously.

"So then you tended me yourself to make amends, and brought me this coffee which smells so delicious. I hope all my enemies will treat me with equal kindness," he said, smiling.

The tight clasped hands relaxed, and her face lit joyfully. "Oh! I do so hope you will like the coffee," she cried. "I made it myself, just as Papa always liked it. And it really was a *kind* of accident — my hitting you I mean. I wouldn't have done it if I'd known who you were. So perhaps it wasn't a very bad lie after all."

There was a wistful note about this, and Charles found himself assuring her that it really wasn't a lie at all, merely a dissimulation, perfectly understandable in the circumstances. Under the spell of those glorious eyes — sunlit hazel they were this morning — he was on the verge of assuring her that he really rather liked being hit over the head, in a perfectly friendly fashion of course. Fortunately, before he committed this final idiocy, she went on eagerly, "If you've truly forgiven me, perhaps you'll permit me to come and talk to you — about Spain

43

and the regiment. There is much that I want to know."

Charles understood that what she really wanted was to hear him speak of her father. The chance of talking with someone who had been near him in the last months of his life might never come again. He did not relish the prospect, but in common decency he could scarcely refuse. He said that it would be very agreeable to have company later on — "when I am a little more presentable for a lady's society," he stipulated, rubbing rueful fingers over his unshaven jaw and suddenly aware of the shocking spectacle he must present, attired as he was in the landlord's nightshirt.

Enjoying a hearty breakfast, he even devoted a few minutes thought to the mystery of Helen Easton's presence, apparently unattended, in this tiny inn. But it was, after all, no business of his. He applied himself instead to consideration of his own dilemma. His pretended disability certainly gave him an excuse for lingering in Springbourne, but it also hampered his personal activities. If he was supposedly incapacitated he could scarcely stroll about the countryside engaging in the sort of casual converse that Mr. Gressingham had suggested.

That the whole community was probably involved in smuggling activities he had little doubt. It was so much a commonplace that the odd thing would be to find someone who wasn't involved. He was not particularly interested in the wholesale apprehension of smugglers — that was a job for the preventives. But somewhere among their venal ranks were the callous traitors who were willing to betray their own countrymen for French gold, the men to whom slitting a throat was no more than wringing a chicken's neck. Sussex born himself, he could not work up much genuine wrath against ordinary smuggling, though he was well aware that it led to violence and crime. Selling information was a very different matter. Lying in his comfortable bed in an English inn, with the sweet airs of an English summer morning drifting over him and an excellent English breakfast inside him, Charles thought of the cheerful indomitable scallywags he had left behind in Spain. The thought that even one of them might be betrayed to his death by the informer he was hoping to unmask made it perfectly possible to summon up some enthusiasm for the task. Indeed he felt capable of doing a little throat slitting on his own account. But lying in bed feigning ill-health wasn't going to get him very far, and he lay awaiting the coming of Giles in a fury of impatience.

When at last the big groom put in an appearance, he was accompanied by his brother, a genial giant of much the same stamp, who had to be presented in form. A few moments were passed pleasantly enough in exchanging views on the recent exploits of *the* Division and in answering Jasie's particular enquiries about old acquaintances in the 52nd. He also enquired, but casually, after his guest's well-being, and grinned over his mishap of the previous evening.

"Aye — well — she's a mettlesome lass is Miss Nell," he submitted, "and she's cause enough to be anxious, so I hope you'll not be too hard on her. Anyway, from what our Giles tells me,

46

she's not done you such a bad turn." He stumped across to the window seat, explaining that his peg leg, while good enough for most jobs, didn't take kindly to overmuch standing. "So if it's all the same to you, Sir, I'll just sit here and keep an eye on things while you tell me what way I can best serve you."

"I told him you were here to make a few enquiries, quiet like, and that maybe he'd be able to give us a few pointers," threw in Giles.

Charles nodded. Mr. Gressingham had urged upon him the need for the utmost caution and secrecy. "Trust no one," he had said. But you would get nowhere without asking questions, and any sensible man must see where the questions were leading. Jasie would have to be trusted with the story, and Charles had a pretty good notion that the trust was not misplaced.

Certainly he had not overestimated the innkeeper's intelligence. He was prompt to offer a practical suggestion. "If it's Bart Rudd at the Fleece that you're nosing after, I'll send along to see if he can let me have a drop of brandy, seeing as how I don't keep suchlike. But with a sick man staying in the house I might be needing it. Young Giles here can take the message. That way he'll get alongside o' Bart, and maybe he'll stumble across something. It's the only way he'd notice it," he added with a fraternal grin at 'young Giles.' "If he doesn't," he went on, ducking away from the cuff aimed at his head and growing serious again, "then you'll have to remove to the Fleece. I'm not a man as has much patience with niffy-naffy invalid fancies, so the Fleece'll be the place for you." He grinned amiably at Charles's indignant face.

"I knew I'd have done better to stay in Spain," growled the ungrateful invalid. "Can you and Giles find me no better employment than to lie here, allowing it to be known that a tap on the head from a schoolgirl has laid me out?"

"Ah, but it won't be known, Sir," smiled Jasie indulgently. "Miss Nell 'ud never let on that an officer of the 52nd could have such a trick served on him."

The reply did nothing to assuage Charles's wrath. Giles, with commendable tact, pointed out that as they had already told Dr. Hilsborough that Captain Trevannion had met with an accident, it wouldn't do to change the tale now.

"And just what fairy tale *did* you tell?" asked Charles sourly.

"Said you'd cracked your head on one of they beams in the parlour," he was told, "and I'm sure it's no wonder if you did, for I've done it myself a time or two. I've often wondered why this great hulking good-for-naught doesn't have the ugly things taken out."

"Just because some folk walk about with their eyes shut — or maybe their skins so full of my good ale that they can't see a lump of solid oak, you'd have me pull my good parlour about, would you?" retorted his brother. "I'll have you know they beams are nigh on a hundred years old. Come out of the *Royal William* when she was broke up. Done more for old England than ever you have, my lad, those beams."

These brotherly recriminations might have continued indefinitely but for Charles's prompt intervention. "I suppose it's a good enough tale," he allowed grudgingly, before Giles could take up his brother's challenge. "Anyway it will have to serve, since, as you say, it won't do to alter it now. You get over to Wintringham then, Giles, and see about this cognac. Tell him it must be the real stuff — that I'll not have any of your Spanish brandy. If he can produce it, then he's either a magician or he's hand in glove with the smugglers."

Jasie looked dubious. "I never heard aught against Bart Rudd," he mentioned thoughtfully. "He's a foreigner in course. Came down from London. Can't say he's a man I take to, but he's affable enough. Nor I never heard of him having any dealings with the 'gentlemen'. Which ain't to say he don't. But I'd have thought to hear about it." And his mild blue eyes regarded Charles with a sly twinkle which indicated that he himself was pretty well informed about the doings of those mysterious 'gentlemen'.

Charles suddenly remembered his own passing thought that it would be the man who wasn't apparently involved in smuggling who would seem out of pattern in the Sussex countryside. The landlord of the Fleece might well repay investigation.

He resolutely resisted Giles's attempts to persuade him to stay in bed. He would play the invalid if he must, but only to the extent of sitting in the rocking chair with a dressing-gown over his shirt and breeches and a patchwork quilt, removed from the bed by Giles, carefully tucked about his resentful limbs. Thus established he felt capable of receiving Miss Easton's promised visit.

She came, rather shyly, just before noon, and perched on the window seat, her expression half friendly half doubtful, and asked him how he did.

"As well as can be expected," said Charles mournfully, and then added, with a rueful twinkle and one hand indicating the bruise over his right ear, "What in the world did you use? A sledge hammer?"

"No. The poker from Emma's bedroom fireplace," said the literal minded Miss Easton solemnly.

"But of course! I recall now that I read in some journal or other that poker work was the very latest fashionable accomplishment for young ladies. I had understood however that the poker was usually heated first, and can only be grateful that on this occasion you omitted that necessary preliminary."

Under his serious gaze her expression changed from solemn wonderment to amused appreciation, and at his final comment she gave a soft little crack of laughter. "You're roasting me," she declared, quite unconscious that the phrase was a little unusual on the lips of a delicately bred young lady. "Papa was used to do that, and with just such a sober face. You are the most complete hand, and I had begun to think you — " she broke off in sudden dismay.

Charles had a very fair idea of what she had started to say. Maliciously — but after all he owed her something for that crack on the head — he repeated gently, "You had begun to think me?"

The girl didn't answer directly, though quick colour flooded her cheeks. Instead she said, "Why are you home on furlough? The division may well be over the Pyrenees by now."

That was a smart recover thought

Charles appreciatively. This soldier's daughter certainly knew the value of a brisk counter attack, even if her social manner left a good deal to be desired. "I was wounded you know," he said softly, watching her face with interest. "Before the poker work," he qualified.

She refused to be amused. "I see," she said, coolly scornful. "It doesn't seem to be a very serious wound." It was clear that she had the poorest opinion of an officer who applied for sick leave on such feeble grounds.

"Also my grandfather died recently, and I have certain business affairs to settle," he offered hopefully.

This did not appear to improve his standing in the lady's eyes. Her attitude remained aloof as she expressed conventional sympathy over the death of his grandfather and then added in a stiff little voice, "It is quite your own affair of course, but I should have thought — " and stopped again.

But Charles had had enough of her half sentences. Also he was discovering in himself an odd desire to stand well with her. "You would have thought that

I'd prefer to be with my regiment. And you are perfectly right of course. Without wishing to appear discourteous, I would, at this moment, infinitely prefer to be in Spain. Unfortunately I was allowed no choice in the matter."

The girl's face cleared, and she said eagerly, "Oh! You were ordered home in fact. Did you bring despatches?"

Charles shook his head, realising the pit he had dug for his own feet. This bright-eyed intelligent child was becoming much too curious. He remembered thankfully that she had been brought up under military discipline. Perhaps that would hold her off. "A soldier obeys his orders. He neither questions them nor discusses them with strangers," he said quellingly.

The outrageous girl actually laughed at him. "Oh! What a horrid set-down," she chuckled. "But I expect I deserved it. Very well. I won't ask you any more. But there are lots of things you could tell me about Spain without broaching military secrecy," she said coaxingly.

This was the inquisition he had dreaded. Hastily he searched his mind for details that he might fitly present to a young girl totally ignorant of the realities of war. It would be difficult, if not impossible, to describe the fall of Badajos without allowing the sheer horror of attack and sack to invade the story, but he must do his best.

"Your father was engaged in the attack on the breach, close by the Santa Maria bastion," he began quietly. "You will know that we were driven back again and again. Every kind of obstacle had been set in our path, and it seemed impossible to make any progress. The men showed incredible courage, attacking time after time in spite of terrible losses. I saw your father once when we had been forced to draw off for a breathing space. He was busy with his men, encouraging them as was his way with sly jests about the enemy. They loved him, you know. And to him they were his children, sometimes wayward but always forgiven. He might tongue-lash them with all the worst names in the language, but they knew how he fought for their rights and comforts."

He hesitated for a moment. Now he must be careful. It could only hurt the child to know how futile her father's death had been, for all the desperate fighting at the breach had been in vain, and the town had eventually fallen to General Picton's 3rd Division. He went on gently, "It was during the last attack that Colonel Easton was killed. Perhaps I should say wounded, though I believe he died almost immediately. He was shot through the breast and was already sinking when Dr. Burke was called to him. I do not think he suffered greatly."

The girl's voice, husky with emotion, said quietly, "So he never knew that the town was won?"

Lie or not, and he couldn't be sure, he spoke it confidently. "I think he must have known. We were over that damned ditch before he was struck, and we all knew that the town must fall."

Her soft lips quivered, and she turned to look out of the window. He could see her pleating and unpleating a crumpled handkerchief. And there was no comfort he could offer. Unless perhaps it would comfort her to know that while the great mass of the slain had been buried in common graves, the Colonel's men had insisted that he be buried with decency and dignity. They had dug his grave themselves and had rendered their last salutes with touching sincerity. He tried to tell of this as calmly as possible, since he himself found it oddly moving. It was too much. With a pathetic little sob she fled, murmuring, in a voice almost choked by tears, "I'm sorry — I cannot — but thank you! Oh thank you!"

5

HE was heartily sick of his own society before relief came. His bedroom was comfortable enough but it offered little in the way of entertainment. A bedroom, at the Lamb, was meant for slumber. Having studied in detail a sampler worked by Emma Thurlow aged nine in 1792, which declared austerely that the only true happiness lay in virtue, he had exhausted the intellectual resources of the room, and since it lay at the back of the inn there was little to be seen from the window. So it was with positive gratitude that he heard the already familiar knock on his door. Miss Easton had quite an individual method of signalling her approach. First came a run of four little taps as each fingertop in turn hit the oak, and then a chord as all four knuckles struck it together.

"Jasie says will you take some refreshment? Giles is not yet back, and it is growing late. If you are hungry there are hot mutton pies, or there is cold beef and cheese and fruit. Jasie is very distressed about not feeding you properly, but to tell the truth they don't often have people putting up here, and without Emma to see to the cooking Jasie is rather at a loss. I told him I was sure you'd be easy to please. If all the tales he tells are true, you must have had far worse food in Spain."

"Acorns and army mule?" asked Charles quizzically. "I can see you have been listening to the usual apocryphal army tales. But it's true enough that good English food tastes like nectar and ambrosia. It's not fitting, though, that you should wait on me, child. Send the little kitchen lass up with it."

"Please let me bring it for you. It is so dull with nothing to do. I like to be busy."

Charles felt sorry for her. In spite of her cheerful manner the traces of tears were still to be seen. He guessed that their earlier interview had been followed by a prolonged bout of weeping. Nor would he be loathe to have a companion to share his temporary prison.

"Then perhaps you will honour me by staying to share the feast?" he suggested.

Her face brightened. "Oh! That would be delightful." And then on a more doubtful note, "if Emma says I may. You see," she confided, "I have only just left school, and Emma says I seem to have no notion how I should go on, now that I am a young lady. Would it be improper, do you think?"

"Of course not," roundly declared Charles, whose notions of propriety were no better schooled than hers. "We shall call it a Picknick — and there can be nothing improper about sharing a Picknick with an old comrade of your father's."

Really the child's face was absurdly transparent he thought, watching doubt, amusement, wistful longing for the offered treat reflected in her eyes.

"I shall tell her so!" she said firmly, and departed hopefully on her errand.

Apparently Emma's verdict was favourable, for very shortly he heard Jasie's uneven tread as he mounted the stairs with a tray. Behind him came Nell, carefully carrying a tankard of ale in one hand and a glass of lemonade in the other. These she set down on the dressing table, and announced cheerfully, "Emma says it is perfectly proper, but that I ought not to have asked you. *That*, it seems, was forward and unbecoming. It is all very difficult. I fear I shall never learn."

Jasie, having set the tray conveniently to hand, took his departure, saying over his shoulder, "I'll send Giles up to you, Sir, as soon as he do come back, and don't let Miss Nell tease you with her cantrips."

Nell glared indignantly at his departing back, but since her small white teeth were at the moment sunk in a particularly luscious peach, found it impossible to express herself with her usual fluency. Having disposed of the peach and wiped her fingers on her napkin, she asked bitterly, "Why is it that people who have known you since you were small can never see that you are now grown up?"

Charles knew better than to answer that one. "He is very fond of you, and proud of you too," he suggested soothingly.

"Oh — as to that, I love him dearly. And Emma. They are darlings. And to speak truth I don't know how I should go on without them. But I do wish sometimes that they would remember that I am seventeen and not seven."

"Have you no relatives who could take you in charge?" asked Charles curiously. "Surely your father cannot have intended you to remain here alone with only servants, however kind and devoted, to care for you?"

"I was to have gone out to Spain to join him," she said sadly. "But when my father was killed, my plans were all at an end. When I left school I came home, but Emma said it wasn't proper for me to live alone, and she and Jasie said I should come here for a while, just until after the baby was born and then they would see what could be contrived."

Charles was more puzzled than ever. "This is not your home then?"

She looked quite startled at such an idea. "Oh no! Mama and I lived at Brockert House. It's about half a mile away. Papa chose it so that Mama could be near Emma and Jasie. He knew they would look after us. The doctors had said that it would be fatal for Mama to undertake the journey to Spain, let alone the hardships of a life spent following the drum. So then Papa bought Brockert House — and I was sent to school at Tunbridge Wells. These peaches are from Brockert House," she added, helping herself to another. "Parfitt sends over a basket of fruit every week."

"Parfitt is your steward?"

She nodded. "And Mrs. Parfitt is the housekeeper. But they are old. Mrs. Parfitt was my mother's nurse. So Emma and Jasie thought I would be safer here."

"Safer?" He uttered the word on a note of surprise. What danger could threaten the girl in peaceful England?

Nell's colour rose. Somehow, since he had talked of her father, she had begun to feel that he was a friend, and she had been chattering on for ever about her private affairs, enjoying the unusual treat of having an understanding listener. She smiled at him in deprecating fashion. "Oh, Jasie has this notion, from what my papa told him — but I daresay it's all a hum — that my wicked uncle might try to dispose of me."

"Your wicked uncle?" Surprise had turned to incredulity, and the girl's face burned with yet deeper colour at the note of amused disbelief.

"Yes. I know it sounds quite fantastical, and more like a page out of a novel than real life. But he really did try to murder my papa. That bit is quite true. But I mustn't be boring on for ever about myself. Even at school we were taught that it was excessively ill-bred to do so. Pray forgive me," and she favoured him with a polite and purely artificial little smile.

Charles felt a brute. The note of hurt dignity in the young voice was rather touching. Though still only half convinced he made haste to offer amends.

"It is for you to forgive me, if you will be so generous. I should not have doubted you. But if you could understand how utterly safe and peaceful England seems after such scenes as I have witnessed in Spain, perhaps you could bring yourself to pardon my amazement."

64

She looked at him steadily. "England isn't always so very safe either," she said quietly. "Only a few weeks ago a young man was found murdered at Wintringham. If one has enemies, no place is safe."

"You are very right, and my disbelief was unpardonable. I hope you mean to show that I am forgiven by going on with your story. Who is your wicked uncle, and why should he wish to dispose of you?"

"He is Sir Nicholas Easton now of course. He succeeded to the baronetcy when my father died. He holds some government post I think. At any rate he lives in London, though the estate is in Yorkshire."

She hesitated here for a little while, as though uncertain whether or not to go on with her story. Charles felt he could scarcely press for her confidences on such brief acquaintance, but heartily hoped that they would be accorded him. So it proved.

Presently she took up the story once more. "I have never seen my father's home. He had never been happy there,

65

and when he joined the army immediately upon leaving Winchester he never went back again. His own mother died when he was born, and his father married again almost at once. It was a great scandal Emma says. It seems that he — my grandfather — had been coerced into marriage with an heiress when he was all the time deep in love with someone else, and no sooner had his first wife died than he married his first love. My Uncle Nicholas is only a year younger than my father."

"They are, in fact, half brothers?"

"Yes. And my uncle was always my grandfather's favourite, and much petted and indulged. It was always Papa who was blamed and punished when the two of them got into mischief."

"And his attempt to murder your father?" prompted Charles.

"That was when he was thirteen and my father fourteen, home from school for the holidays. Uncle Nicholas offered to show him a guillemot's nest on the cliff. Papa said it couldn't be, because guillemots didn't breed on the coast there, but my uncle vowed that it was.

66

So the two of them set out early in the morning and climbed down the cliff to the ledge where the nest was supposed to be. My papa was in front because the ledge was too narrow for them to change places and Uncle Nicholas said he wanted him to see the nest properly. They came to the place where the ledge narrowed to nothing. Papa could see no sign of a nest, nor any bird droppings on the rock, so he said, 'Where is it then?' And Uncle Nicholas said, 'There is no nest, you fool,' and he pushed Papa over the cliff."

"Good God in heaven!" exclaimed Charles, so carried away by the impact of this simple tale that he forgot to guard his tongue.

"That's attempted murder isn't it?"

Charles nodded. "It certainly is. But your father survived. And what happened to your uncle when the story came out?"

"It didn't come out. Papa fell on to a ledge lower down the cliff. He lay there insensible for hours. When he came to himself he found that his leg was broken and he was not able to help himself.

He didn't even know if the place was above high tide or not. The searchers sent out by his father did not find him till next morning. During the hours of that night he determined to say nothing about his brother's part in his fall. He knew that he would never be believed. But he never forgot. And when he went out to Spain he had Jasie promise that if — " she stopped for a moment, then went on determinedly, "Jasie promised that neither my mother nor I should ever be left to the tender mercies of my Uncle Nicholas. My papa saved Jasie's life you see — after Corunna — so it was a debt that Jasie was glad to pay."

"Yes. I see," said Charles slowly. "But why should your uncle wish to be rid of you? Had you been a boy it would have been understandable. But now — he has the title and the estate — what harm can you do him?"

"The money," she explained simply. "My grandmother's fortune was tied up in a trust for her children. My grandfather had only a life interest. At his death it went to my father, and now to me. And until I marry, my uncle is my heir."

"Is there no one on your mother's side of the family who could give you a home? You ought to be thinking about making your debut and parties of pleasure and pretty clothes," he said, with vague memories of his sister's excitement over these matters.

She shrugged. "I haven't thought much about such things. My whole heart was set on joining Papa in Spain. But there is no one — at least no one of the kind you mean, who could arrange for my presentation. There is an elderly aunt of Mama's who lives in Dublin. Jasie is of the opinion that I might make my home with her. He thinks it would be safer. But Emma says Dublin would be no better than exile, and very little safer than Sussex. She says that there are ladies of rank and consideration who could be persuaded to take me in charge for a suitable recompense, and that it is just a matter of choosing the right one and deciding how best she should be approached."

She spoke quite calmly and impersonally, apparently unaware of the picture of desolation that she was painting. Charles was moved to deep compassion.

"There will be no difficulty about that," he said cheerfully. "I would have suggested that you should go to my sister, save that she, too, is in an interesting way, which makes such a scheme ineligible just now. Perhaps my aunt — but no, you might not be happy with her. She is a very high stickler, with an inflated notion of what is due to her consequence. But I can think of several ladies, wives or mothers of your father's friends, who would, I am sure, gladly offer you a home for his sake. And that would be much more comfortable for you. You need not think of going to strangers."

"You are very kind to concern yourself with my affairs," she said shyly, "especially after the way I treated you last night," she added, a naughty twinkle dispelling the gravity of her expression. "I wasn't very polite to you this morning either. Truth to tell, I thought you were shamming it, and making out to be much worse than you were."

"Where in the world did you pick up such a shocking vocabulary, Miss Easton?" demanded Charles, anxious to divert her attention from this all too accurate estimate of his state of health. "You will certainly set society by the ears if you use such phrases."

"I am aware — " and she smiled at him quite enchantingly — "but I know I need not mind my tongue with you, sir, since you certainly swore in front of me just now, which is much worse."

Charles had to laugh and admit that she was quite right, and the dangerous topic was successfully skirted as Miss Easton began to enunciate mischievously the collection of army slang and cant terms with which she had been accustomed to shock her teachers and delight her schoolmates. She had not nearly exhausted an extensive and most reprehensible repertoire when Giles put in a belated appearance, rather shocked to find his master rocking with laughter and much too obviously in the best of health and spirits.

"'Tis easy to see you're much improved, Sir," he remarked dryly, and bent to pick up the patchwork quilt which Charles had early discarded and forgotten all about. "Just so's we don't have you

71

in high fever by nightfall getting so excited, and you with a head wound scarce healed," he added in significant tones, scowling at his master from behind Nell's back.

"Do stop fussing, Giles. You sound like an anxious nursemaid," retorted his ungrateful charge. "Laughing never hurt anyone. Tell me — did your errand prosper?"

"Yes and no, you might say, Sir. I had speech with the landlord, but he has no brandy he says. Seemingly you can only lay hold of *that* if you have an arrangement with the free traders. Which in course he hasn't. Or so he says. Very polite and full of regrets he was, to have to be so disobliging. He can offer you a nice smooth port he says, and the Madeira's fair enough. He has rum too, if you've a fancy for a drop of punch. But never a drop of brandy."

"Is that Bart Rudd?" asked Nell. "I expect he was lying. He's a horrible man. I don't know about his dealings with the free traders, but I'm sure he bullies that poor woman who keeps house for him. He won't even let her go to Church or make friends with any of the village women."

"That'll be the niece," agreed Giles thoughtfully. "She served me with a pint of ale and a bit of bread and cheese. She did seem a miserable down-trodden piece. But never mind for that. Just as I was for making back to report, there's a chaise pulls up and a fine town gentleman gets out of it. Real slap up to the echo he was. Been there before too, 'cos he calls the stable lad by his name, which is Jim. And since he brought a cloak bag with him, which young Jim carries into the house, it seems as how he's for stopping. Name of Sir Nicholas Easton, and he was enquiring the way to Brockert House."

6

NELL came slowly to her feet. The merriment which had lit her face died away, and her pretty colour faded. For a moment no one spoke. Then Charles said cheerfully, "Excellent. Now we shall see where we stand."

The girl gazed at him blankly, her quick wits still dazed by the suddenness of the shock.

"Don't you see?" explained Charles, "if there really is danger, your uncle can do nothing openly. It would never serve if any so-called accident that might befall you could be traced to his agency. So when he is openly enquiring for you, you are safe. What we must guard against is any attempt to remove you from the keeping of your friends to — let us say — his Yorkshire home, where you would be much more vulnerable. Now tell me — who is your legal guardian?"

She looked bewildered. "I don't think I

have one. There are trustees who manage my money affairs — my father's lawyer is one of them — and he has always paid my school bills and my allowance. But that is not the same thing is it?"

He shook his head. "Unless your father left a will appointing a guardian for the period of your minority, we could find ourselves in a very awkward situation."

She looked at him trustfully. "In what way?"

"I very much fear that your Uncle Nicholas, as your nearest male relative, could claim rights of guardianship."

Her eyes widened and darkened. "I'll never submit to such an iniquity. Do you mean that he could dictate where I should live and how I should behave?"

"I'm afraid so," nodded Charles ruefully. "Until you marry. And no doubt his consent would be necessary before you *could* marry. But come — we are looking at troubles that may not exist. We don't know but that your father named some perfectly suitable guardian for you. So cheer up, my child. After all — you are not quite friendless."

One small hand flew out to touch his

arm fleetingly in an impulsive gesture of gratitude. She even managed a smile, though it was rather a tremulous one. "If you will hold me excused, I think I should at once tell Jasie of this newest happening," she said quietly.

"Aye — you do that, Miss Nell. I'll lay he'll be more than a match for your uncle. Or if he isn't, Emma will be," said Giles, moving to open the door for her and casting a darkling frown on Charles's attempt to forestall him.

"Had you forgot that you're a sick man, Sir?" he enquired, a touch of acerbity underlying the soft Sussex drawl. "That wench is no dafthead. She's bound to see you're up to something."

"The poor child has troubles enough of her own without concerning herself with my affairs," said Charles pityingly. "But no matter for that just now. What did you make of the innkeeper?"

"Too smooth and too helpful by half," said Giles bluntly. "And as for him having naught to do with smugglers, I don't believe that either. He's some reason for keeping his dealings dark, and that's a mighty suspicious thing, for no honest Sussex man would think the worse of him for it. What's more, he took good care that I'd no chance of a private word with Jim Cooke — that's the stable lad I mentioned. Jim might just to say have let it out that they *did* have dealings with the free traders." He shook his head ponderously. "It's sure there's something havey cavey about him, but whether it's what we're after is a different matter. You'll have to take a fancy to a drop of his port. That'll give me a chance to go over again."

Charles groaned. "Port! As though the headache I've got isn't enough! Now. What about this uncle of Miss Easton's? He's been here before you say? Could he be concerned in our affair?"

Giles stared at him. "Nay Sir!" he said reproachfully, "A brother of Colonel Easton's?"

"Half brother," corrected Charles briskly. "And a thorough-paced scoundrel from what I can make out, or so the colonel himself thought."

Giles scratched his ear thoughtfully. "It's possible it's just about Miss Nell. Depends how long he's been coming about these parts."

Charles nodded. "Yes. But one thing we can reckon on. It's business of one kind or another that brings him, for there's naught in Wintringham to bring a man of fashion out of town on pleasure bent. What's more, Miss Easton says he's employed in government service. That would fit too."

There was a thoughtful silence. Then Giles shook his head slowly.

"Straws, master, just straws," he grunted.

"True enough," agreed Charles grimly, "but given enough straws, one begins to make bricks."

"So parson used to tell us," grinned Giles. "Well, Sir, we'd best make it the Madeira, since you don't fancy the port. And maybe I'll manage a word with young Jim. All agape I'll be, about visitor, chaise, horses and all. Never seen such afore in all my puff. I reckon he'll be proud to tell me all about 'em, including how regular they come."

Further elaboration on this simple method of extracting information was interrupted by Bella, who bobbed a curtsey and nervously rolled the corner of her apron round one hand as she announced breathlessly, "If you please, Sir, Mistress Woodstead 'ud be glad if you could step along and have a word with her, if convenient." Having delivered herself of which painstakingly acquired message, she turned and fled.

Charles quirked an eyebrow at his ally. "She might at least have offered to conduct me to Mistress Woodstead's room," he said. "I own myself most eager to meet your good sister-in-law."

"It'll be to do with Miss Nell's affair. Emma thinks as much of Miss Nell as if she was her own flesh and blood. Which is natural, seeing as she's brought her up from a baby. She'll be worritting herself to flinders about this uncle coming down hereabouts. As for her quarters — they're just a step across the landing from your door."

When Nell had said that even Papa was a little afraid of Emma, Charles had pictured a tough and strapping female, a regular Amazon, an image based on some of the camp-followers who had accompanied the army in Spain. But the woman who greeted him with quiet dignity as she sat propped against her pillows, was quite unlike the creature of his imagining. She was probably in her early thirties, for her skin was fresh and smooth and there was no trace of grey in the smooth bands of brown hair that showed beneath her beautifully laundered cap. She put down the sewing on which she had been engaged, settled her shawl more closely about her shoulders, and leaned back against the pillows, her hands lying relaxed in her lap and her calm grey eyes studying him with a cool concentration that was curiously impersonal. Under that clear measuring gaze Charles began to feel quite uneasy — a sensation almost unknown since nursery days. He found himself actually stammering a little as he murmured polite enquiries as to Mistress Woodstead's health and the well-being of her small son, peacefully asleep in a wooden cradle standing near the hearth.

She waved his courtesies aside, not rudely, but as one who had no time to waste on trivialities, and gestured to him take the chair which had been set beside the bed. Meekly Charles did so.

The room was over warm, for even on this summer day a low fire was burning. Perhaps this was why he felt an impulse to run a finger around a neckcloth which suddenly seemed too tight.

"I am much obliged to you for coming, Captain Trevannion. I want to beg your help for Miss Easton. Jasie says 'tis a great impudence on my part, and there's no call to tease you with her affairs. But you've served with Colonel Easton, and I think you'll not desert his child in her need."

Her softly accented country voice fell pleasantly, soothingly, on his ears. It was so serenely assured that he would naturally do his duty as she saw it, that he found himself, almost before he was aware, assuring her that he would be honoured to serve Miss Easton in any way that she could suggest.

At this she smiled at him quite delightfully, so that he was able to sun himself in her approval. He wondered whether to mention his own tentative ideas for Miss Easton's future, but since his hostess seemed to have fallen into a gentle reverie it was perhaps more courteous to wait for her to resume the conversation.

Presently she sat up erect, nodded briskly as though her thoughts had reached a satisfactory conclusion, and with her head tilted a little to one side offered him her lovely smile again and said, "You will forgive my bluntness, Sir, but time presses. From what Giles tells me, I understand you to be a single gentleman. Have you any female relatives to whom we could entrust Miss Nell?"

So her plan was the same as his. Quite pleased, Charles smiled back at her. Really, with her head at that angle, she reminded him irresistibly of a very intelligent terrier at an unusually promising rat hole. There was nothing in the least intimidating about her after all.

"I never before regretted my lack of female relatives, ma'am. I am, as you say, unmarried. And I have only the one sister who, as it happens, is in a delicate situation just now. I had been thinking of the wives of some of our senior officers, almost any one of whom would be happy to take Miss Easton for her father's sake. But it would take some little time to arrange, and time, as you say, presses."

"Then is there any lady of good standing — the mother or aunt perhaps of some young lady of your acquaintance — to whom we could appeal?"

Charles shook his head. "I'm afraid my acquaintance is almost entirely masculine," he said apologetically. "Military duties leave one little time for social engagements." He looked up, caught a derisory gleam in the grey eyes, and capitulated completely. "And are much more to my taste," he confessed, grinning.

She smiled back; that wonderful, understanding maternal smile. "In that case, the best thing you can do is to make Miss Nell an offer," she said gently.

For a moment Charles scarcely realised the import of her remark. He was still savouring the satisfaction of having so easily made friends with the redoubtable Emma, of whom 'even Papa was a little bit afraid.' The shock of comprehension was all the greater. Could he have heard aright? Had the incredible creature really made that preposterous suggestion, just as though it were the most natural thing in the world?

And she was laughing at him. "Pray don't look so frightened!" she begged. "Oh dear! Jasie has always said that my enjoyment of the ridiculous would be my undoing. But if only you could see your own face! I don't mean you to *marry* her! But you could give us good cause for holding out against Sir Nicholas when he seeks to take her from us. Which he will do," she went on, seeing Charles still bereft of speech, "for well I know the Colonel never writ anything down, dear careless man that he was, always one to put off doing the dull tasks till next day."

"Even if I were to consent to such an outrageous scheme," said Charles, already half convinced that this mad-brained goddess was in the right of it, "will you ever get Miss Easton to agree to it?"

Again that piercingly sweet beneficent smile. "As to that, Master Charles, I'll rely on you to persuade her. She's just the least mite wary of my management."

As well she might be, thought 'Master

Charles' never even noticing that he himself had been reduced to nurseling status by his unconscious acceptance of the childhood title.

"It will be best," explained his mentor, "if you settle it between you right away. The Parfitts were instructed to tell any callers that Miss Easton was visiting friends in the neighbourhood, but it hasn't been possible to keep the child close hidden, and any number of people will be able to advise Sir Nicholas of her whereabouts. There may not be very much time to think of a credible story. Fortunately Sir Nicholas can know nothing about you, or how recent is your acquaintance with your 'betrothed'. At least — " with sudden anxiety — "you do not know him, do you?"

Charles shook his head reassuringly.

"Then it should be possible to convince him that your friendship is of long standing and that the betrothal had Sir Jonathan's approval. We shall say that you are to escort Miss Nell to your sister's house as soon as I am sufficiently recovered to accompany her."

"And if he remains in the neighbourhood?

We can scarcely hope to maintain such a deception for more than a few days."

"Oh — by then we shall think of something else. You will find Miss Nell in the herb garden. I asked her to pick the lavender while the sun was on it. It is good for the hands to be busy when the mind is anxious. I am sure that you will be able to bring her to a proper understanding." And she nodded gentle dismissal.

7

"NO," said Nell firmly. "I could not do it."

Charles ran a hand through his already wildly ruffled locks, and returned to the attack. "You need say nothing yourself," he pointed out. "I will engage myself to apprise your uncle of the situation. All you have to do is to acquiesce."

"But it's all lies," she persisted. "And when I know it to be false, acquiescence is as bad as telling the lies myself. I know Papa would say so."

"And would he also say that you must meekly submit to your uncle's guardianship?" reminded Charles grimly.

"Of course not. But I must think of some way out that does not involve me in deceit. You must *never* lie for your own advantage," she ended, as one reciting a well learned lesson.

Sudden inspiration visited Charles. Perhaps after all there was a way out of the impasse. "Could you bring yourself to accept the scheme if it were not to advantage yourself, but to help me?" he asked.

She lifted a surprised face to his. "How would it help you?" she said doubtfully.

"It could do so," he answered, "but if I am to explain how, I must tell you a little more of my purpose here, and I must be able to rely absolutely on your discretion."

Perplexity and doubt were swept from her expressive countenance, and eagerly she assured him that she would be discretion itself. Charles had little faith in the discretion of any female, but after all he need not tell her very much.

"In the pursuance of my orders," he picked his words with care, "it is necessary that I remain in this district for a while. And since my true purpose is secret, I must have an obvious and convincing reason for so doing. It seemed at first that my — er — accident might serve the purpose. Unfortunately it also limits my usefulness, since if I am supposed to be laid on a bed of pain I cannot move freely about the village. This scheme of Mistress Woodstead's would suit admirably, for no one would think it at all odd that I should wait to escort you both to my sister's house when we are supposedly betrothed."

Nell was wavering. "Yes — I can understand that. And though I cannot like the scheme, yet if it would serve you — "

Charles played his final trump. "It would indeed serve me. But remember too, if such deceit is distasteful to you, that in helping me you are also, serving England."

As he had hoped, this argument proved to be a clincher. From positive aversion she began to display modest enthusiasm, and by the time they had worked out the details of their imaginary acquaintance, it must be regretfully confessed that a youthful delight in play acting had quite overcome any remaining moral scruples. Once convinced and committed she proved a far more ingenious conspirator than Charles, inventing a romantic story of their first meeting, which, she decided, had taken place at Shorncliffe. The ten year old Nell had taken a tumble — "And that's true enough," she interjected, "for it was for ever happening. I had an ambition at that time to ride one of my father's horses, Conqueror, a splendid chestnut, and since he wouldn't accept a side saddle I rode him with just a blanket strapped on him till Emma found out. She was so angry with me she actually reported me to Papa. He gave me a tremendous trimming for daring to ride his horse without permission, but he wasn't really cross. Indeed I heard him telling Jasie afterwards that I was pluck to the backbone and should have been born a boy."

She broke off abruptly, colouring furiously, and put her fingers over her mouth in a gesture of dismay. "Oh dear!" The gay young voice dropped to a repentent murmur. "That was boasting wasn't it? Papa would have been disgusted if he had heard me."

"No such thing," contradicted Charles briskly. "He would still be proud of your pluck — but if he could see how charmingly you look, he would be glad he had such a pretty daughter instead of a son."

As a compliment it was rather a clumsy effort, but Charles had had little opportunity of practising the art of turning a smooth phrase. Nell heard it with interest. "Do you really think I'm pretty?" she asked hopefully, "or are you just practising to impress my uncle? I suppose, if we are betrothed, that you will have to pay me compliments."

"That will be my pleasure," declared Charles, improving rapidly.

"It's a delightful pastime," agreed the lady cheerfully. "I like to hear you say charming things, even if it is only a game. But where was I? Oh yes! Conqueror had just thrown me. And a tall and handsome young ensign came to my assistance. I can pay compliments too, you see, she said with demure mischief. "From that day I became most deeply attached to my gallant rescuer," she went on with a fine dramatic flourish, "And so — and — oh dear! What comes next?"

"Why, when I was on furlough eighteen months ago," improvised Charles, determined not to be outdone, "I visited my Godmother who resides in Tunbridge Wells, and chanced to accompany her to church. Judge of my surprise when, among the bevy of young ladies from the local seminary — which one was it, by the way? Miss Pringle's? — I recognised my youthful sweetheart, now grown to a damsel of surpassing beauty. Whereupon I fell headlong in love."

The 'damsel of surpassing beauty' eyed him with considerable respect, and said reverently, "It's a splendid story, isn't it? Only I'm afraid now we have to be serious. I don't like to bring darling Papa into such a farrago of nonsense, though he would have dearly enjoyed the joke, but I think we must say that on rejoining your regiment you made it your business to become better acquainted with him, and at last approached him with a request for my hand in marriage."

Better to finish the tale on a light-hearted note, thought Charles, and plunged boldly on, "And he, well aware that with my natural genius I must inevitably end up as a Field Marshal, naturally snatched at such an excellent match for his only daughter. He was, of course, already cognisant of my domestic virtues, having frequently shared the suppers of acorns and army mule with which I was so apt to entertain my friends. Such a paragon is rare. He could scarcely be blamed for accepting such an eligible offer on your behalf."

He regarded his 'betrothed', submerged in helpless giggles, with an air of languid disdain. "Really, ma'am," he drawled affectedly, surveying her through an imaginary quizzing glass, "this ill-timed mirth is not becoming to my future bride. And that is another thought," he went on, with an abrupt reversion to his normal manner. "If we are supposedly betrothed I can scarcely continue to address you as Ma'am or Miss Easton. What may I call you?"

She looked up at him a little shyly. "My name is Helen, but Papa always called me Nell. He said that Helen only led men on to destruction — I collect that he was referring to Trojan Helen — but Nell, he was used to say, was merry and kind. It would be comfortable if you would call me Nell. Should I address you as Captain Trevannion or as Sir Charles?"

"If you can bring yourself to do so, I

believe you should address me as Charles, perhaps even," he teased wickedly, "as dear Charles, or dearest Charles."

She primmed up her mouth reprovingly. "I am sure it would be most improper in me to use such affectionate terms in public," she said firmly, "so it will not be necessary for me to practise them."

"But seriously," he rejoined, "I think we should try to maintain our roles even when we are alone." Seeing her instinctive recoil he added hastily, "I was only jesting, of course, about the way you should address me, but do pray bear in mind that it is not only your uncle whom we wish to impress. We want everyone to accept our story, and we cannot always be assured of our present privacy."

"Yes. Of course," said Nell thoughtfully. "You know it is all very well inventing a romantic tale, but I am afraid I do not know how I should behave. You see" — half laughing, half shy — "I was never betrothed before."

"I must confess equal ignorance," admitted Charles. "Perhaps Mistress Woodstead will tell us how we should go on. Meanwhile I think it would present a pleasing picture if I were to carry the basket while you finish picking the lavender. I am sure they behave just so in Arcady — and can only regret that my attire is not more appropriate to the setting."

But Nell, looking fondly at his well worn uniform coat, declared that the satins and ribbons of Arcady could never be so becoming to a man as was a soldier's coat.

"Certainly not so comfortable," added Charles. "I sometimes wonder how I shall do when this campaign is ended."

"You will sell out?"

"Not till we have done with Bonaparte of course. Perhaps not then. Though I doubt if I'd enjoy a soldier's life in peace time. It is difficult to remember a time when we were not at war, or to imagine a life spent in administering one's estates."

"Do you inherit then? You mentioned your grandfather's death, but I thought — " and she stopped, blushing at the impertinence of her question. But Charles was not offended. Indeed since they must necessarily be much in each other's company, he was thankful to find her so natural and conversible.

"Like you, I am an orphan," he explained, answering her unspoken query first. "So I do, in fact, inherit. Trevannions is quite a small estate though. I doubt if there would be enough work to keep me occupied. And my grandfather's steward has run the place ever since my father was killed."

"Oh! Was your father also a soldier?" asked Nell eagerly.

He had said too much. But too late to poker up now, for he could not possibly snub this nice confiding child. "No," he said quietly, "he was killed in a duel. I am afraid it is a most unhappy story. My mother had been brought up in Barbados in the West Indian islands and had never left that sunny clime until she married. She and my father were deep in love, but unfortunately my mother never settled in Sussex. The cold shrivelled her up, she was used to declare, the houses were both stuffy and draughty, and the sun never really shone. Nevertheless she endured these rigours patiently until, at the time of my sister's marriage she

96

chanced to meet a young man whom she had known as a child in her island home. I have always believed that it was only a nostalgia for the scenes of her girlhood that made her value his company, for he was ten years younger than she. But she was heedless, too trusting in her friendship. The affair became an open scandal, and the outcome was a duel in which my father was killed outright and his opponent so seriously wounded that he died within the month. Overwhelmed by the tragedy which she had brought upon us all, my mother fled, returning to her old home and, so my grandfather subsequently informed me, dying of a fever while I was still at school. Don't look so sorrowful, child. It is an old story now, and grieves me only that I was never able to seek my mother out as I had planned to do."

In the centre of the garden was an ancient sundial. They had drifted towards it as they talked and Nell had seated herself on the worn stone at its foot, her head studiously bent over the lavender in her lap, while Charles leaned one elbow on the dial itself, tracing the scorings on the stone with an idle finger. The sun was still gilding the crumbling stone though the shadows were growing longer. A small hand slid gently into the battle hardened palm that hung lax at his side. A quick warm pressure and it was gone, so swiftly that he might have dreamed it, but the girl's low voice roused him to present reality. "Just a schoolboy — perhaps the same age as my father was when he was so cruelly hurt. But at least your sorrow was caused by misunderstanding and not by deliberate treachery."

The loss of both his parents, and the circumstances which inhibited its discussion, had raised a barrier between a sensitive boy and his contemporaries, so that he had withdrawn into himself, pleasant but aloof, trusting no one wholly save Giles who had won his place before tragedy struck. It had cost him an effort even now to speak openly and calmly as he had done to the girl at his feet, yet the telling, after all these years, had brought a sense of peace. Perhaps there was a magic of healing in that sun-soaked herb-scented garden. Certainly he felt strangely refreshed.

He smiled down at the shining dark head bowed so assiduously over the sprigs of blossom, and though she did not see the smile Nell could hear the lightening in his voice as he went on, "And indeed I do not know why I should be boring on for ever with tales of old griefs. Though doubtless" — and now for sure he was teasing — "when you are betrothed to a gentleman on such short acquaintance it is as well to learn all you can of his family history. My great-grandfather, for instance, was a very dirty dish. *He* made Cornwall too hot to hold him at the beginning of the last century. It is generally understood that he laid the foundation of his fortune by pursuing a successful career as a wrecker."

"What is that?" asked Nell, seconding his obvious wish to bring the conversation to lighter topics.

"It is a pastime peculiar to isolated and savage sea coasts. By displaying false leading lights, especially during rough weather, it is possible to lure the unsuspecting mariner into dangerous waters, where in all probability his vessel will become a total wreck, to the great profit of the wreckers."

"But what happened to the sailors? Were they not brought into great danger?"

"I fear so. Indeed it is said that such as survived the onslaught of the seas were often very roughly handled if they did manage to struggle ashore."

"What dreadful wickedness! Of course it all happened long ago," she added hastily, suddenly realising that she was passing these severe strictures on his forebears.

"Many years ago," he agreed solemnly. "I do not think that I can justifiably be blamed for my great-grandpapa's conduct. And even at his worst, he never, so far as I am aware, attempted to push his elder brother over a cliff. Certainly he cannot have succeeded in doing so, since there are still Trevannions living in the original family home in Cornwall. Perfectly respectable people I believe," he added gravely, "though I have never had the pleasure of making their acquaintance. *They* still remember great-grandpapa you see."

Nell giggled. "And having founded his

fortunes and earned the opprobrium of his neighbours, he removed to Sussex?" she enquired.

"There to purchase an ancient and ruinous manor house, which he caused to be pulled down, and several adjacent farms. He rebuilt the house, but for one reason or another was never able to settle on just the name to give it. Hence, being generally described by his neighbours at Trevannion's place, it came by its present name — Trevannions. He later married the younger daughter of a neighbouring landowner, and settled down to a life of dignity and consequence. He even became a magistrate. Quite a reformed character you see."

Nell shook her head regretfully. "I am afraid that my ancestors are a very dull lot. None of them seem to have done anything exciting."

"Exciting people are not necessarily pleasant to live with," Charles pointed out. "You certainly have a rather unusual uncle. And if I am not mistaken he is about to pay us a visit. From Giles's description of it, that can only be his chaise. He is certainly not one to let the grass grow under his feet. I had not expected him until tomorrow. Now do we go into the parlour to meet him? No, I think not. We will permit him to seek us out here, for certainly in this pleasant spot we must present a picture of idyllic happiness."

He searched his fellow conspirator's face for signs of undue nervousness, but was well satisfied with what he saw. Her expression was perhaps a little set but her colour was natural and there was a militant sparkle in her eyes. Feeling his gaze upon her she looked up at him enquiringly. He smiled at her — and Charles's rare smile was delightful. "That's my good girl," he said cheerfully. "Chin up — Nell!"

8

THE gentleman who stood surveying the scene from the doorway of the inn appeared to have little taste for the Arcadian idyllic. His brows had creased slightly at the sight of the couple in the garden, though he had already been informed of the presence of a military gentleman at the Lamb. Now, as he saw the girl smile up into the officer's face, saw the fellow actually set his fingers under her chin and stoop as though to kiss her, the crease deepened to a scowl and he strode forward a pace, only to check at once. He had not, for years, permitted himself to act upon impulse. The situation was not quite what he had expected to find, but he had no doubt of his ability to handle it to his own satisfaction. Undoubtedly, until he found out exactly how the land lay, his best approach was one of avuncular concern for the welfare of an orphaned niece. So it was with lips curved in an agreeable smile that he strolled forward and bowed gracefully to the young lady.

"Miss Easton? Miss Helen Easton?" he enquired in soft cultured tones.

Nell was rather taken aback. Somehow she had built up the picture of a regular villain, of the type she had frequently encountered in forbidden novels. The eminently presentable gentleman bowing before her bore no resemblance to the creature of her imagining. His air was assured and easy, his dress immaculate. She could see nothing to cavil at there, though to the more worldly Charles it spoke eloquently of town life and was unsuited for country wear. To crown everything he was undeniably handsome, his colouring dark, his features clear cut, and his figure good, apart from a slight tendency to fleshiness natural in a man of sedentary occupation.

Yet Nell found herself regarding him with a revulsion that had nothing to do with her knowledge of his past. Later, when she had time to sort out her impressions, she was to decide that it was the smooth impassivity of the face that was so repellent. It was almost mask-like in its calm. The smile which curved his mouth did not warm his eyes. Whatever thoughts and emotions stirred behind the mask were not permitted to wrinkle its smooth surface. To Nell, herself a creature of impulse and as transparent as glass, he seemed slightly inhuman and a little frightening.

She curtsied slightly at his address and said composedly, "Yes, sir. That is my name."

"Then may I be permitted to present myself? I am your father's younger brother — your Uncle Nicholas."

She curtsied again, this time with a touch of cool hauteur, but did not speak. In dealing with the enemy — and that Sir Nicholas was the enemy she had no doubt whatever — it was quite unnecessary to subscribe to social conventions. They could dispense with small talk.

Sir Nicholas seemed unperturbed by his chilly reception. "You may have heard my brother speak of me, my child," he went on kindly. "I have not presumed to intrude earlier on your grief, since I knew that you were well cared for in the seminary where my dear brother placed you. But now that the time has come for you to take your place in society you will need help and guidance. I can, of course, produce proof that I am indeed your uncle if you so desire."

"My father told me a good deal about his half brother," said Nell, with some emphasis on the 'half'. "I cannot see any family resemblance, but I don't doubt that you are indeed Sir Nicholas Easton."

"Then perhaps you will consent to be private with me, since there are certain family matters to be discussed between us. Pray hold the lady used, sir," he added, bowing politely to Charles.

"Present me to your uncle, Nell, if you please," said that gentleman quietly.

"Why yes — if you wish it — " she murmured with an air of mild surprise at such a request. "Captain Sir Charles Trevannion, of the 52nd. Regiment, Sir Nicholas Easton of Scarroby in Yorkshire, my father's half brother."

The gentlemen exchanged slight formal bows.

"And now — may we be private, niece?" repeated Sir Nicholas. "Time presses, for already it is evening and there are many arrangements to be made."

"No need for privacy, sir," said Charles cheerfully. "Nell and I have no secrets from each other. You could not know it of course, since you have only just found us out, but we are betrothed, and plan to be married soon. You may count me quite one of the family."

The privilege seemed to give Sir Nicholas little satisfaction. "You cannot be serious," he said in deeply shocked accents. "Marriage plans so soon! Not for anything would I wish to appear censorious, but I am sadly grieved to find you wearing colours, my dear. To have put off your half mourning so soon seems to indicate a lack of sensibility that I can only deplore."

Nell's eyes flashed fury. "My father expressly forbade us to wear mourning if — if — in the event of his death. No one, he said, should mourn for a soldier killed in the execution of his duty. They should be proud — as I am, sir."

Since this was certainly unanswerable, Sir Nicholas continued smoothly as though she had not spoken. "Nor can

I approve your residing in this — er — hostelry," turning upon the humble Lamb a critical eye, "quite unchaperoned and, to make matters worse, in company with your affianced husband. It is really shocking." He turned reproachful eyes on Charles. "You, sir, have been about the world, and must be well aware that such conduct is most improper. Consider the slur that your heedlessness casts on the fair name of this innocent child! Why — if it were to become known there is not a lady in good society who would receive her. *My* niece!"

This reflection appeared to move him beyond speech, for he fell silent, obviously brooding over the shocking behaviour of the younger generation and their total lack of consideration for the susceptibilities of their elders.

"No slur can possibly rest upon Miss Easton's good name," said Charles very softly. "If any such suggestion is made, I shall know very well how to deal with it. In the present instance it is quite absurd. Miss Easton has been all the time in the care of her devoted servants. As for my own presence here, since you are a relative of Miss Easton's, and so in some measure entitled to concern yourself with her welfare, I am willing to explain. Shortly after my arrival here last night I met with a slight accident and sustained a trivial injury which made it impossible for me to remove from the inn. If however this explanation does not satisfy you — " He shrugged, and allowed the sentence to trail away, his eyes bright and hopeful.

But Sir Nicholas, it appeared, was not yet ready to force an issue. He ignored the scarcely veiled challenge, bowed acknowledgement, and remarked coldly, "I am happy to see that your health is now fully restored. I apprehend that you will be leaving Springbourne very shortly?"

"No," said Charles steadily. "I have decided to wait till I can escort Miss Easton to my sister's house, where she is to reside until our marriage can be arranged. I daresay Mistress Woodstead will be able to undertake the journey, perhaps a month from now."

This news apparently dealt Sir Nicholas a shattering blow. He positively groaned as he shook his head over such shocking depravity. "It cannot be, young man. I really cannot permit such scandalous laxity. Helen, pack such things as you will require for the night. You must place yourself under my protection at once. How extremely fortunate that I decided to come in my chaise instead of riding over, as was my first intention. I shall carry you back with me to the Fleece this very day. The rest of your gear may be sent after you. We can only trust that this very foolish lapse will never be discovered. I take it that you can rely on the loyalty of your servants. And you, sir, can be discreet I trust?" He glared fiercely at Charles.

Charles smiled at him affably. "Why — as to that, Sir Nicholas, it has never been tested," he said pleasantly. "Nor is like to be now. I do not share your opinion that you are Miss Easton's natural guardian. As her affianced husband, the care, both of her person and of her reputation is my privilege — and my pleasure," he added, with a slight bow in Nell's direction. "But since we are not agreed on this point, perhaps it would be better if we discussed it more privately. Nell, my dear, would you not like to take this lavender to Mistress Woodstead? You must be weary of all this brangling."

She met his eyes squarely, her face a little pale, her slim body tense but her voice quite composed as she said, "I think Sir Nicholas is in the right of it, dear Charles. In our joy over our reunion we have been careless of convention. I have been sadly at fault and must beg your pardon, but while you lay senseless I could think of nothing but my prayers for your recovery. I see now that I have been betrayed by my anxiety into conduct unbecoming to my position."

What the devil was the wench about, thought Charles furiously. This was not the course they had agreed upon. But she had cut the ground from under his feet. "Why, my love — if you are quite sure that this is what you wish — it shall be so. But I must inform you," he went on, trying to sound suitably arch and playful, "that when we are wed, I shall expect obedience to *my* wishes. This, you must know, is the duty of a wife."

What a thrice damned fool I must sound, he thought idly. And then, at once, good thing if *he* thinks so. But what sort of a game was the girl playing? He'd be willing to stake his inheritance that she was terrified of her uncle. He'd seen that frisson of revulsion run over her too expressive countenance. So why submit to his wishes without cause?

"When we are married I shall naturally obey you in all things," said Nell in a submissive tone wholly belied by the dimple at the corner of her mouth. "Meanwhile Sir Nicholas will not wish to keep his horses waiting for ever." She moved towards the inn door, Sir Nicholas following close behind her.

Charles went off to the stable yard, where, as he had hoped, he found Giles peacefully engaged in setting a few stitches into a well worn saddle. A brief colloquy ensuing, the groom nodded, put aside his task and turned to the stall where the big Andalusian was housed. Charles strolled back to the inn and after a few words with Jasie in the taproom made his way to his bedroom where, in a matter of five minutes he had gathered together his few belongings and packed them in his valise.

In the pretty room that Emma had set aside for her use Nell sat down in the windowseat to write a note to Charles while Bella started to pack her portmanteau. After hesitating for a full minute over the delicate question of how best to address him, she remembered that she must make haste lest Sir Nicholas grow suspicious and wrote hastily without preamble of any kind: "I saw well what you had in mind, but I could not let you fall into argument which might lead to a duel. You are not to be fighting my battles. But our compact may still hold, for I beg you not to desert me but to remain in the neighbourhood. I will not remove from the Fleece without informing you. Pray do not be anxious for me. I shall have my pistol." Having signed this effusion and sealed it with a wafer, she instructed Bella to give it to Giles, asking him to hand it to his master privately. "Don't let Sir Nicholas see it," she urged, "and come back to me when you have delivered it safely."

The girl went off, goggle-eyed with excitement at taking part in what she felt sure was a secret assignation. Nell turned to the folding of delicate muslins, too fragile to be entrusted to Bella's willing but clumsy hands, her face a little wistful as she stooped to the task. He had accepted her decision so easily, never guessing what it had cost her in sheer cold courage. Perhaps he had thought her reassured by her uncle's respectable appearance. She shivered, and remembered another task which could not be left to Bella. From a locked drawer in the bureau she took the case that held her pistol. She would have to find time to load it, a task which needed care. Not here and now with Bella's return imminent. Swiftly she hid the case at the bottom of the portmanteau and closed the lid. Bella was taking an age, and Sir Nicholas would be growing impatient. She would go and bid farewell to Emma and the baby, then she could truthfully say that this had delayed her. It was so very much easier to tell the truth, as well as more comfortable. Play acting was fun though, she decided with a reminiscent smile as she went down the passage.

The good-byes were not so painful as she had expected. Emma was brisk and cheerful, vowing that her sojourn at the Fleece would be brief, and recommending her to put her trust in Captain Trevannion, "a good sort of a man, and one that will bring you safe off from this tangle by one way or another."

Sounds suggestive of a cart horse hastening home proclaimed the return of Bella, and brought Emma's admonitions to an abrupt close. "That wench!" she sighed despairingly. "The times I've told her! Now you be off, Miss Nell, and try not to fret too much for the outcome. You're in good hands with the Captain, and Jasie and me'll keep an eye on things too, so's Sir Nicholas'll not dare try any tricks with all of us watching."

Nell kissed her lightly and went quickly out of the room, fearful of betraying that she was not feeling near so brave as she could wish. Bella, breathless with haste, was standing just inside her bedroom. "I'm ever so sorry, Miss, I'm sure," she panted. "I couldn't find Mr. Giles anywhere, but he do be come back now. Been on an errand for Sir Charles. I give him the letter like you said, and he says as he'll give it to his master."

Nell thanked her prettily for her services, and then indicated a gay shawl lying on the bed, saying that she had no further use for it but thought the colour might be becoming to her attendant. Bella clasped the shawl lovingly to her breast and expressed sincere if incoherent gratitude. There was no further excuse for lingering. Nell put on her hat, and accompanied by the ecstatic Bella carrying the portmanteau, made her way to the parlour.

Sir Nicholas was pacing the floor, watch in hand — an unnecessary gesture of petulance, since the wall clock kept good time. He strove however to conceal his irritation, smiling at her with a gleam of well preserved teeth which reminded her forcibly of the nursery tale of Red Riding Hood, and making jocular comment on the time it took young ladies to prepare for a journey.

Much against her natural inclination Nell meekly begged pardon for the long delay, explained that she had been taking leave of Emma and baby Giles — "my God-son" — and walked out to the waiting chaise."

Here however there was another unexpected delay. Leaning against the mounting block, all the leisure in the world in his indolent pose but coming gracefully to his full height as his 'betrothed' reached his side, was Captain Trevannion, attired now in riding clothes.

"Ah! Here you are at last, my dear," he greeted her cheerfully, unconsciously echoing Sir Nicholas's strictures. "You went off in such haste that I had no opportunity to ask you about the mare. Shall Giles bring her over to the Fleece, or do you prefer to keep her here? It is so short a distance that it makes small odds."

Since she had no mare, nor indeed any kind of mount stabled at the Lamb, Nell found herself in a puzzle. Which did he want her to say? Then it seemed obvious that he was showing her an easy means of keeping in touch. With a mount stabled at the Lamb, messages could pass between them easily and naturally.

"Here, I think," she decided eventually. "She's such a nervous creature and might fret in strange stables."

The quirk of Charles's lips assured her that she had chosen aright and that her quick perception had amused and pleased him. Emboldened, she went on, "Need we forego the ride we had planned for tomorrow? Sir Nicholas can have no objection to that," clearly she intimated that he had better not, "since your groom will be with us. I will have Bella pack my habit, for I had forgot that I should need it. Will you call for me at — say — ten o'clock?"

"Giles shall certainly bring the mare over at that hour," said Charles pleasantly. "For myself, of course, I am coming with you now. I sent Giles off at once to bespeak me a room at the Fleece, and fortunately the landlord was able to accommodate me. I did not quite like to tear Giles away from his family so soon," he went on apologetically. "He can easily bring the horses over whenever we need them."

He bowed politely to Sir Nicholas. "I shall be honoured to escort your chaise,

118

sir," he smiled. Then, turning to hand Nell into the carriage he explained kindly, "There can be no food for scandal, you know, in my putting up at the Fleece, since Sir Nicholas himself will be there" — deliberately and mischievously he used the Spanish term — "to play duenna."

9

IT was fortunate that Charles was riding behind the chaise, thought Nell, or it would have been difficult to contain the bubbling merriment within her. Her spirits had gone bounding up when he had so calmly announced his intention of sharing her exile at the Fleece. For the moment Sir Nicholas no longer seemed a sinister and potent threat. Charles had made him look slightly ridiculous, and so reduced his villainous stature. The ordeal she had braced herself to face had suddenly become a gay adventure, for Charles was sharing it with her. She wished she were riding with him instead of being cooped up in this stuffy vehicle, but at least she could look forward to a good gallop tomorrow.

Sir Nicholas made no attempt to engage her in conversation during the brief drive that carried them to Wintringham. He surveyed the passing rural scene without visible emotion, and when they reached their destination handed her over to Miss Smithson without further ceremony. Since Charles had gone off to see to the stabling of his horse there was nothing to do but accept Miss Smithson's offer to show her the three available rooms so that she might choose the one she preferred. There was in fact little to choose between them. All were spotlessly clean if simply furnished. She chose eventually a small room at the back of the inn, looking out over the stable yard into a small paddock with an orchard beyond.

Miss Smithson showed mild surprise at her choice, but admitted that it would be quieter than the two larger rooms that fronted the highway and were above the public rooms. Nell did not care to confess, even to herself, that she had chosen as she did because her window might afford an occasional stolen glimpse of Charles, for it was natural to suppose that with Giles left behind at Springbourne he would oversee the welfare of his horse in person. Instead she endeavoured to engage Miss Smithson in conversation. It was not a very rewarding occupation. Miss Smithson, though polite almost to servility, was monosyllabic and depressing. In appearance she was scrupulously neat but colourless, every scrap of hair tucked away under her cap, her complexion pale, her eyes a dull grey. Only once did she show any sign of animation, and this was when Nell chanced to refer to Emma. At this there came a gleam of interest in the lacklustre eyes, and she enquired earnestly after Mistress Woodstead's health. Eagerly Nell began to explain that Emma was her own kind nurse and dear friend. It seemed as though they might reach a better understanding when a thump on the door announced the arrival of Nell's portmanteau. The lad who dumped it unceremoniously inside the room informed Miss Smithson that the master was wanting her and seeking her everywhere. She seemed to shrink a little, muttered her excuses to Nell, and hurried out of the room.

Nell went about her unpacking soberly with a smile only for the shaking out of her habit, slightly creased from its hurried last minute inclusion by unpractised hands. It was actually rather a shabby garment, old and a little faded, and she hoped that she would be able to get into it, since it had been made for her before she had done growing.

Then there was the problem of finding a safe hiding place for the pistol case. A brief examination convinced her that there was no such place in the room, and she was eventually forced to conceal the case at the bottom of her workbag, where it lay snug beneath the innocent white cambric folds of baby Giles's robe. Tonight, when everyone was in bed and there was no danger of interruption, she would essay the ticklish task of loading. A glance at the door had already shown that the key was in the lock, and she now walked across and tried it. It turned easily and smoothly. Whatever Miss Smithson's shortcomings as a conversationalist she appeared to be an efficient housekeeper.

The rest of the evening passed quietly enough. After dinner — a simple meal offering little choice of dishes but well cooked and piping hot — Sir Nicholas had withdrawn to a side table and immersed himself in a mass of papers, but presently he emerged from his abstraction to address himself to his niece. "I had hoped to have carried you to Town within the sennight, my dear, for I am sure your aunt and cousin are all eagerness to welcome you, but I fear this tiresome business is like to detain me longer than I had thought. However I daresay you will not repine, since you have Captain Trevannion to bear you company," and he bestowed a gracious smile upon Charles.

Nell was staring at him in frank astonishment. Until that moment she had thought him to be a bachelor. "My, cousin, sir?" she enquired. "I did not know I had a cousin."

"Did you not? My Robin is seven years old. Too young I fear to be a companion to you. But my wife will be very glad of your coming. She is of a delicate constitution and does not go much into society, so that the inclusion of a young female in our family circle will be great comfort to her. I promise you that they are both quite agog at the prospect of your coming."

There seemed to be no adequate answer to this, since Nell was not disposed to perjure herself with protestations of equal enthusiasm. She did however acknowledge that as she had Captain Trevannion to ride with her she was not likely to find a prolonged sojourn at the Fleece in the least tedious.

"What a veritable Diana you are, my dear," sighed Sir Nicholas. "Now have I that right, I wonder? My schooldays are, alas, so far behind me, but I seem to recall that Diana was the Goddess of the chase. Certainly she is associated in my mind with horses. One would describe an accomplished horseman as a Centaur, but one can scarcely apply this term to a young lady I feel."

Since neither of his companions seemed disposed to enlarge on this theme, he sighed plaintively, as one whose creditable efforts to furnish suitable small talk were not meeting with the success that they deserved, and lapsed into a gentle melancholy from which he was only shaken when Charles enquired, "How long do you expect to be detained here, sir? For as soon as Mistress Woodstead is able to undertake the journey I intend, as I informed you, to escort Miss Easton to my sister's house where she is to stay until such time as we can be married."

Sir Nicholas frowned. "I cannot approve such a scheme," he said austerely. "So hasty a plunge into matrimony gives an extremely off appearance. My niece should first be presented to society by her aunt, and there should be no thought of a wedding until she has been granted the opportunity to look about her a little. As for my own plans," he went on, his manner mellowing a little, "I cannot be sure how long I may be kept dangling here. I am concerned with settling up the estate of my wife's aunt who died recently. She has been something of a recluse, and her affairs are in such chaos that it seems like to take longer than I had first imagined."

"My own affairs will not permit of undue delay," Charles said firmly. "My furlough is not unlimited, and I, too, have much to see to in connection with my grandfather's estate. I wait only to see Miss Easton safely lodged with my sister."

"On the matter of an early marriage we are unlikely to reach agreement," said Sir Nicholas mildly. "I am persuaded, dear child, that a little rational thought will convince you of the impropriety of such conduct. To be married in such haste must cause even the most charitably minded to look askance, while what will be said by persons of less benevolent disposition is quite unthinkable."

Nell found it oddly difficult to refute his arguments. She was almost grateful when he suggested that it might be better if she withdrew her 'charming presence' for a little while, leaving the gentlemen to discuss the matter more freely.

Sir Nicholas, having helped himself with polished grace to a pinch of snuff, appeared to be considerably refreshed, for he shrugged off his habitual languor and said quite crisply, "Now sir. Let us have this out without further roundaboutation. I have sent an express to my poor brother's lawyers enquiring whether I am named as guardian in his Will. Until I hear from them I am assuming the duties of the child's natural protector, as I am sure Jonathan would have wished.

My niece is a minor, and she is also a considerable heiress. I do not know if my brother favoured this match, but if I have anything to say in the matter, I shall need to know a good deal more about your circumstances before I can consent to it. I intend no disparagement of your birth or character, but a military man is not the husband I would choose for a delicately nurtured girl. I must be fully assured that the dear child has every prospect of comfort and happiness before I can lend my support to your pretensions."

The man was really wasted off the stage, Charles decided. He sounded so sincerely concerned that it would have been quite a pity to spoil the touching scene by suggesting that his support had not been asked. As well in any case that Sir Nicholas should think him wholly deceived. Politely he bowed his understanding. "I must acknowledge that your attitude is perfectly reasonable," he said gravely, "though I trust I shall be able to allay your doubts without undue difficulty once I am assured that you are indeed Miss Easton's legal guardian. I shall await the outcome of your enquiries

128

with impatience."

Since there was really no more to be said Sir Nicholas returned to his voluminous correspondence. Charles chose rather to stroll out of doors in the evening coolness of the tiny garden, where presently he was joined by Nell who had caught a glimpse of his tall figure through the window of the Fleece's rather grim little parlour.

"What did he say?" she demanded eagerly.

Charles shrugged. "Nothing of consequence. Just that he cannot like your marrying a soldier."

Nell tossed her head scornfully. "He doesn't know me. If we were really going to be married, that would be the best part of it. I have always longed to follow the drum. No stupid insipid parties, or minding my tongue and my manners which I'm sure I should never remember to do."

The corners of Charles's mouth twitched. "Madame, you grieve me to the heart," he said mournfully. "Can it be that my obvious and manifold charms have failed to touch your maiden fancy?

That my only attraction in your eyes is that I could offer you a passport to scenes of violence in a dashed uncomfortable and much over-rated peninsula?"

Nell gave a little gurgle of laughter. "Since you fully intend to cry off as soon as is convenient to you," she retorted, "you cannot even command my respect, much less my maiden fancy. Besides I know that gentlemen do not understand. Even my papa was used to say that women were a curst nuisance with the army."

Charles nodded. "Though I might phrase it more courteously in your presence, I am wholly in agreement with him. The tail of an army is no place for a gently bred female."

"I told you gentlemen didn't understand. If I were married to a soldier I could not endure to be left behind. How could one bear to be safe and comfortable at home, to wear fine clothes and go to parties, and even flirt with other gentlemen, because I know that fashionable ladies do so, and to know all the time that one's husband was probably cold and hungry, perhaps even wounded, with not so much as a comfortable pillow for his head?"

But Charles shook his head, saying soberly, "Think of the other side of it, my child. How could a man do his work with all his mind and strength, how could he go into battle, knowing that the wife whom he had vowed to cherish was exposed to deadly danger through his own selfishness in keeping her at his side? And believe me, war is not romantic. The days of chivalry are done. There may be deathless courage on the battlefield — I have seen it — but there's a deal of dirt and pain and loss. And when a city is sacked — if you had seen — " He broke off abruptly. "But I should not be speaking of such things. What matters more at the moment is that Sir Nicholas says he has sent to discover whether he is your guardian under your father's will. It must be several days before he can expect an answer, but you should be on your guard. He is quite capable of producing some authentic looking document in an attempt to trick you into submission to his wishes. Since you are all so sure that your father would never have committed you to his care, it may well be that you will find yourself a ward of court. That would afford you some degree of protection."

Nell understood very little of this legal phraseology, but if Charles said it was a good thing, she was prepared to accept his dictum. She found deep comfort in a growing conviction that her new ally would not lightly desert her, so that it was in a reasonably cheerful frame of mind that she retired to her room to the promised refreshment of a glass of warm milk, Sir Nicholas having pronounced that the tea served in these parts was quite undrinkable.

In spite of the mildness of the summer night a tiny fire had been kindled in her bedchamber, and though its warmth was superfluous its gay little flames were cheerful. The glass of milk, carefully wrapped, was standing on the hearth. She sipped it distastefully. She had never really liked milk, and determined in future to ask for coffee or chocolate. It was growing late. By the time that she had loaded the pistol and tucked it back into the workbag, she was quite thankful to prepare for bed.

But her sleep was restless and broken and she woke early to hear the grandfather clock on the turn of the stairs strike six. For a little while she lay relaxed, trying to recapture the comfort of drowsy forgetfulness, but it was no good. Sundry small sounds from the yard below announced that others were astir. There was the clink of pails and the sound of a horse's hoofs. Feeling ever more wide awake, she finally decided to get up and go for a walk.

A rather scrambling toilet sufficed. She would make good deficiencies when she came back. She pushed open the casement and leaned out, considering the several paths that she might take and finally deciding on the one that led through the orchard, a decision not uninfluenced by the idea that ripe cherries would make an agreeable start to her explorations. Just below her window she noticed as she drew in her head, was a mounting block. It would have been almost possible to have made her exit from the inn by this unorthodox route. A year or two ago she would not have hesitated. Nowadays she thought sadly, feeling positively decrepit, the thought of ripped muslin and bedraggled petticoats was sufficient to restrain her, even if the impropriety of such behaviour was not. She turned her back on temptation and went sedately along the corridor and down the staircase to the front door. The little maid, busily scrubbing the steps, gave her a shy good morning as she went by, but there was no other sign of life about the inn's frontage.

The orchard proved quite as rewarding as she had hoped. There were betraying stains about her lips and fingers when she finally left its confines and wandered down the lane that led towards Springbourne. And presently she found a companion. There was a rustling and a heaving in the overgrown ditch that bordered the lane, and a chestnut red head appeared followed, after another upheaval, by the shoulders and forepaws of a half grown setter pup. He was a friendly creature with most engaging ways, and to judge by the broken cord dangling from his neck, he too was playing truant. He lolloped happily towards Nell, flinging mud and water over her skirts. His legs were disgracefully mired and clotted, but his plumy flag of a tail waved in delighted circles at their meeting. It was impossible, mud or no mud, to repulse such a confiding fellow, and Nell made much of him, fondling the nobly domed head that shone almost blood red in the early sunlight, and petting his silken ears. He invited her to a game of stick retrieving, laughing up at her open mouthed each time he laid the trophy at her feet.

When, however, she wished to resume her strolling progress, the puppy dissented. There were, he assured her, far more attractive scents to be savoured towards Wintringham. She left him snuffling joyfully on some tantalising trail, and walked on towards Springbourne, her thoughts pleasantly concerned with the personality and provenance of the mare that was to arrive, as by magic, for her to ride this morning. She must be coming from Trevannions, some six miles distant, for without even considering the matter she was perfectly well aware that Charles would never put her up on some unknown, untried hireling. She supposed that Giles must have brought her over from Trevannions the previous evening.

It was time to be making her way back, for she would have to put off her muddied dress before breakfast. It was a great nuisance that she could not immediately change into her riding habit, but no doubt Sir Nicholas would take exception to such casual behaviour. Besides, the habit was shabby, and not so becoming as she would wish. She really must make arrangements to be measured for a new one.

A bridle path diverged promisingly from the lane, veering back towards Wintringham. It meandered gently towards the crest of a low hill crowned by a clump of beeches, and should, she estimated, if her father's teaching stood her in good stead, bring her out within two or three hundred yards of the inn. Forsaking the lane she climbed towards the modest summit. It was rougher walking than the lane, the dry turf deeply pitted by hoof marks, and the ascent steeper than it looked. Nor were her light sandals really suitable for such conditions. She grew warm and breathless, and was glad to rest a moment in the shade of the beech trees when she at last reached them. Her calculations, she was pleased to observe, had been quite accurate. Below her and a little to her left lay the Fleece. She had approached it from a fresh angle which presented her with an end-on view. It really made a charming picture she decided, viewing it critically from her vantage point on the hill. The gable end had been recently whitewashed and a climbing rose was flaunting heavy pink blooms against the whiteness. The windows twinkled in the sun, and the side door stood invitingly ajar. From it a cobbled path ran between low clipped hedges to a willow fringed duck pond. An old grey horse grazing beside an uptilted cart at the water's edge completed the pastoral scene. It was a pity, thought Nell, that she had no aptitude for water colour sketching, for this was just the sort of picture that her more gifted friends loved to commit to paper.

But even as she gazed, the placidity of the scene was roughly shattered. An agitated squawking, audible even at that range, broke out from under the willows.

The old grey horse raised his head to stare for a minute, then lumbered off to seek a more peaceful spot, and the stocky, aproned figure of the landlord appeared in the open doorway. At this point the cause of all the commotion passed briefly across the field of Nell's vision. It was her friend of the ditch, now in hot pursuit of the ducks. No doubt the rivulet he had been investigating drained into the pond and so had led him naturally to the point where a new and utterly delightful pastime presented itself to his eager energy.

"Oh! You bad boy!" Nell smiled to herself, and watched to see what would happen. She could hear the landlord shouting angrily at the dog, which rather understandably paid no heed, being now within inches of the madly paddling brood. Even as she realised that the landlord had stopped shouting and gone into the inn, she saw the dog hurl itself half out of the water and seize the nearest duck. She felt apprehensive. Bart Rudd was not likely to be merciful to a strange dog found raiding his duck pond. Certainly her mischievous young friend must be punished, but he was only a puppy and knew no better. Without realising it she began to run, with some idea of averting a punishment that might be out of all proportion to the sin. It was too late. The innkeeper had emerged once more. Standing beside the cart, one hand resting on its framework and the other held out to the dog, he was calling to it in commanding but friendly tones very different from his earlier shouting. The dog, trusting as ever, and obviously quite unaware of any crime, was advancing towards him with difficulty, his progress impeded by the heavy duck which he was carrying, his tail waving in triumph. He laid the duck at the landlord's feet and looked up at him, just as he had done at Nell. The duck got up and waddled hastily away, apparently unharmed. Nell sighed her relief. The dog turned its head to watch the duck, and the landlord's hand came away from the cart frame holding a heavy iron bar which he brought down with all his strength on the silken head which Nell had caressed. There was no sound, though she felt for a moment that she must close her ears to the horrible crunching of the shattered skull and the dying scream that had never been uttered. The splendid body, so eloquent of joyous living, lay in a limp huddle at the landlord's feet, and even as she watched, unable to drag her gaze away, the man stopped and caught it up by the neck, the legs trailing pathetically as he went round the corner of the building and out of sight.

10

A WAVE of nausea swept over her. When she closed her eyes she could still see that sprawled shape. She clenched her hands, trying to fight down the sickness that threatened to defeat her. Then footsteps came crashing along the path behind her, and she heard through her sick daze Charles's voice calling, "Nell! Are you here?"

She turned towards him blindly, her hands going out in unconscious appeal. Charles stared at her in shocked dismay. Having been advised by the little serving maid that she had seen the young lady walking down the Springbourne road, he had set out to meet her, and not seeing her on the road had taken the fairly obvious bridle path. Coming up behind her he had seen nothing of what had occurred, but the look on her face was all too familiar to him. He had seen just such a look of sickened disbelief on the faces of young raw troops brought face to face for the first time with violent death. What in heaven's name, he thought, observing now her mudstained dress and generally dishevelled appearance, had befallen her?

Then she was in his arms, her small hands beating frantically at his breast, great tears raining down her cheeks as she sobbed out some disjointed phrase of which the only words he could make out were, 'to kill him like that,' and something about 'friendly' and 'trusting'. Seriously perturbed and wondering what in the world the child had seen, Charles petted and soothed her back to coherence, holding her cradled against him in one arm while he mopped up her tears with his handkerchief and murmured sundry foolish endearments which later made him blush to remember.

He was considerably relieved when at last he managed to extract the story from a pathetically drooping girl, quiet now save for an occasional shuddering sob, for he had feared that she had stumbled unwittingly into the skein of murder and treachery that lay somewhere close at hand. He managed however to hide his relief, knowing that in her present state any attempt to make light of the incident would only convict him of heartlessness without in any way comforting her: Nor must he be too sympathetic. What she needed was bracing — something to give her thoughts another direction.

"Come now, my child, you've cried enough. Remember you're a soldier's daughter, and we have work to do," he said kindly but firmly. She responded instinctively, drawing herself away from his supporting arm and searching for her own handkerchief to remove the last traces of the storm of tears.

He allowed her a brief space to recover her composure, then went on comfortingly, "Try not to grieve too much over the dog. Remember he cannot have suffered. To be snuffed out instantly at the height of his vigorous youth is not so bad a fate. Many a wounded soldier has wished it had been his."

Nell sighed. "Must I stay in that man's house? I'm sure I can never bring myself to speak to him."

"I will explain that you saw from a distance his dealings with the dog, and that it has distressed you. Which is perfectly understandable. It will give you a reason for avoiding him, and you will be well advised to do so, for I believe him to be a very dangerous man. Now — we must go back before Sir Nicholas misses us and develops further moral scruples."

They left the sheltering beeches and walked down the path towards the inn. "I trust that this sorry start to the day has not given you a dislike for the scheme of riding with me," suggested Charles tentatively. "If you do not feel able for it I shall quite understand, but we shall have few enough opportunities for private converse, and there are several matters to be discussed."

"I wouldn't forego it for anything," said Nell with convincing warmth. "I have been thinking about it this morning, and wondering about the mare. If she has any tricks you had better warn me. A nice thing it would be if she were to put me off under Sir Nicholas's nose, such old friends as we are supposed to be. And I have not ridden for some months and am sadly out of practice."

"From Giles's accounts of your early prowess I doubt if even my Marquis would put you off," returned Charles, thankful to see some of the animation returning to the woebegone little face, "and certainly Martina would not. She is the gentlest creature, with perfect manners, though she dearly loves a frolic if you are in the mood."

"She sounds perfectly delightful. Is Giles bringing her over from Trevannions?"

"He went over for her last night, so that she could get accustomed to her strange stable," he teased gently, and was rewarded by a little smile.

"Is not Martina an odd name for a horse? I am sure I have never heard it before."

"She is out of my grandfather's stud," explained Charles. "All of them have names that begin with MAR, to signify their descent from his great stallion, Mars. The two I have with me are Marshall and Marquis. But actually the lady you are to ride is generally known as Tina, and it will be more natural for you to call her so." He went on talking gently of the horses and their names and personalities, of the bay Andalusian, Galoon, who liked a drink of ale, and such anecdotes as he could recall that were fit for a lady's ears, and presently had the satisfaction of having her converse naturally without her earlier palpable efforts. Entering the inn was clearly an ordeal, but she faced it steadily, and by a fortunate chance she was able to make good her retreat to her own room without encountering either her uncle or the landlord.

Charles made his way into the coffee room where he found Sir Nicholas already at breakfast. To his polite greeting the baronet returned a cool nod and continued his application to the cold beef. Nor did Charles's explanation of the reason for Nell's tardy appearance seem to affect his appetite. He went on calmly consuming his breakfast, and not until he had done justice to the beef and was pouring himself a cup of coffee did he offer any comment on the tale. Then he said indifferently, "I have little patience with such sickly sentiment as females are wont to indulge in. If the brute was killing his poultry, Rudd did very right to knock it on the head. I daresay she will get over it," and proceeded to drink his coffee, walking over to the window embrasure to do so, which permitted him to turn his back on Charles and so preclude the need for any further conversation.

When Nell finally appeared, with a murmured apology for her lateness, he offered no comment, merely saying that he was driving into Rye on business later in the morning, but presumed that she did not wish to accompany him. Nell only wished that he would set off at once, so that she might be free of the constraint of his presence. She was aware that her face still showed traces of tears, and she was having some difficulty in choking down a morsel of bread and butter. The hot coffee was good though. It steadied her, and soothed the ache of weeping in her throat. And Charles, in the intervals of eating his own breakfast, produced a sufficient flow of casual remarks to cover her silence, and managed eventually to draw her into a discussion of a suitable route for their morning's ride. Even Sir Nicholas contributed his mite towards this topic, saying that he understood there was a very pretty ride along towards

Pett, which he was sure they would much enjoy if it was not too far for a lady.

Nevertheless it was with relief that Nell left the breakfast table and went to put on her riding dress. The sound of horses clattering over the cobblestones in the yard brought her to the casement. There was Giles riding the big bay and leading the mare, a beautiful creature with a coat like black silk. Hastily she resumed her struggles with the tight habit, then crammed on her hat, snatched up her whip and ran downstairs. The mare and the Andalusian were hitched to rings in the mounting block and Giles was busy over Marquis in the stable. She could hear the murmur of the men's deep voices as she walked across to the mare. Black ears pricked forward and soft dark eyes regarded her with intelligent interest as she put up a hand to pat the smooth neck. The mare blew gustily at her, tossed her head a little, then apparently decided to make overtures of friendship, dropping her soft muzzle on the girl's shoulder.

"Tina," said Nell contentedly, the morning's grief temporarily forgotten, "my lovely, lovely girl. Oh! Aren't you just a beauty!"

"Poor Galoon is quite cast in the shade," said Charles's voice behind her. "Haven't you a word to spare for him? And how about Marquis here? He also appreciates a little attention."

As the Andalusian chose this moment to utter a derisive snort, and Marquis to look down his rather Roman nose with a very superior air, the simple remark seemed exquisitely humorous to Nell, and it was in a ripple of merriment that she permitted Charles to toss her up into the saddle.

To the watching eyes of Sir Nicholas the little cavalcade trotting gently down the lane appeared entirely carefree and harmless. With the faintest possible shrug, as of one who disclaimed all responsibility, he strolled across to the fireplace and tugged the bell.

It was some minutes before Rudd answered the summons, but Sir Nicholas remained unruffled. Not until the innkeeper, thrusting a hand inside the breast of his coat, pulled out a slim package and laid it on the table, did he display any emotion. Then a shade of annoyance was apparent as he said sharply, "He did not come?"

"Oh yes, he came all right," returned the innkeeper grimly. "But he didn't bring no money. They're not buying any more. Seemingly they're having every kind of trouble over there since the Russian business. What with raising fresh troops and fitting them out, there's no gold to spare for the likes of — us." Little enough of the gold had come his way, he thought resentfully, considering the risks he ran. He must do Sir Nicholas's bidding, for Sir Nicholas knew too much about him to be gainsaid, but he'd have done it more willing if he'd been well greased in the fist. As it was, there was even a mild entertainment in seeing my fine gentleman so nicely thwarted, though he hastily suppressed any sign of amusement as he saw the black rage which contorted Sir Nicholas's features.

But that visible flare of fury was brief. The habit of impassivity was deeply engrained, and within moments he had resumed its mantle. "Then there's no help for it," he said quite gently, "it will have to be the girl. I would rather have waited longer. Her demise so soon after coming under my protection may occasion unwelcome comment. But my affairs will not wait. If only this business had gone through successfully" — he pushed aside the rejected package — "I could have kept to the original plan. Now there is no time to waste on establishing myself as a devoted guardian. I have, perhaps, a month before my creditors become uncomfortably pressing. So let us devise a little."

He glanced enquiringly at Rudd, but quick thinking was not that worthy's forte. "You said it could be made to look haccidental," he growled, "and it's got to says I, for there was too many damned nosey fellows came down on us enquiring into that other young chap's death. I've no mind to swing for the sake of you winning a fortune."

Sir Nicholas regarded him pensively. Threats were no use in this case. A man can only hang once. Therefore he must be persuaded. "There's fortune enough for us both," he said mildly, "and neither of us need swing if we move carefully."

"Aye. And how do I make sure I get my rights in this 'ere fortune you're making so free with?" demanded the innkeeper suspiciously.

"Why, my good man," responded Sir Nicholas airily, "you will know so much about my means of acquiring that fortune that I feel sure I could never resist any reasonable demands that you might make. You see I happen to share your aversion to — er — swinging."

Rudd uttered a surly grunt. His doubts were not entirely allayed, but he was prepared to listen further, and to lend his aid — on terms.

"This damned interfering soldier comes very mal à propos," decided Sir Nicholas thoughtfully. "He would certainly regard the sudden death of his betrothed wife with considerable suspicion, and this we must at all costs avoid. Let us consider if his presence cannot be turned to good account."

He began to pace up and down the room, meditating aloud in short considered phrases, punctuated by intervals of pacing. "I feel, I really feel, that we must dispense with this young man," he

152

began. "I find him quite superfluous. It should not be difficult. If need be — a duel. Only yesterday he was all too willing. But even with my skill, there is always the element of chance about a duel, so we reserve the idea. Some mishap must befall him. An encounter with footpads? A brush with smugglers? Housebreakers would be safer of course, but that sets the scene too close for safety. We must consider this."

He considered it for several moments, pacing backward and forward, and it became apparent that no immediate and perfect solution had been vouchsafed.

"Once we have decided the manner of his disposal, the rest follows naturally and inevitably," he went on. "Heart-broken at the death of her beloved, unable to face a future so bereft, my poor niece commits suicide." A trace of artistic satisfaction coloured his voice as he brought this tragic tale to its dénouement. But Mr. Rudd's withers were unwrung. Indeed he entered a sturdy objection.

"Now that's what I call downright wasteful," he said "The wench is a tasty piece for them as likes them young and tender. There be stews as 'ud give thee a good price for her, aye, and make sure she was never heard of again. Not London, mebbe — that's happen a bit too close — but I've heard tell of some rare places in Liverpool."

Sir Nicholas regarded him with some sympathy, but found himself nevertheless bound to depress this burgeoning hope of easy profit.

"I fear you have not given sufficient thought to the matter," he said kindly, "or you would have realised that I must produce indisputable evidence of my niece's death before I can inherit my brother's fortune. A simple disappearance is not sufficient. There must be ample proof of death, and for this a corpse is the most readily acceptable. It does indeed seem wasteful, but the greater ultimate profit should be our goal rather than the immediate but paltry relief of necessity."

Rudd relinquished his hopeful scheme with regret, but felt bound to admit that Sir Nicholas had a good headpiece on him. "And 'ow was you thinking a young lass would do the dreadful deed?" he enquired, and by way of helpful illustration drew an imaginary knife across his throat.

"Indeed no," replied Sir Nicholas austerely. "It is a well known fact that females cannot abide blood. Nor are they sufficiently skilled in the use of a knife, even if they had the will. No. I think she will rather take poison," he decided reflectively. "We have good authority in literature for such an action."

Rudd eyed him with grudging respect. He would cheerfully knock the girl on the head if so required, but these fancy touches were beyond him. He did however venture to suggest deferentially, "It's queer stuff, Sir, is poison. If you give 'em enough to do the job right, like as not they taste something queer and spew it out. Then you've all to do again, and them suspicious like into the bargain."

"There is much in what you say," allowed Sir Nicholas judicially. "Yet it could be contrived. A small dose of the drug, sufficient to cause unconsciousness, could be administered in coffee or chocolate which would mask the flavour."

"Aye! That's the way of it," agreed his lieutenant enthusiastically. "And then drop her over the cliff before she comes round."

Sir Nicholas frowned sharply and suddenly, a most unusual departure from his customary imperturbability. "No! We'll make sure before she goes over," he said grimly. And added, in a whisper incomprehensible to his associate, "We'll make very sure — this time."

11

THE morning's ride had been a pure delight once they had shaken off the constriction that seemed to charge the atmosphere of the Fleece. The mare had shown herself a perfect mount and Nell had been wholly absorbed in the joy of riding such a responsive yet spirited creature. Once he had satisfied himself that she was fully capable of handling Tina, Charles had left her to her own devices, falling in amicably with her choice of route and watching with interest and approbation as she tested the mare's capabilities. Finally she had led him a merry dance cross-country, in which the lightly burdened Tina had outpaced even the long-striding Marquis, while poor Galoon was hopelessly left behind. When they finally reined in to the gentle amble which permitted conversation, she was quite herself again, eager to dilate on Tina's manifold perfections and even to bestow a meed of praise on the powerful black which he was himself bestriding.

When she had finally done praising the horses, they had fallen into a companionable silence, each pursuing a train of thought which concerned the other. Presently Nell said seriously, "I have no wish to pry into your private affairs and duties, Sir Charles, but I have been unable to keep myself from pondering the probable reasons for your presence here. You said this morning that there were several matters that you wished to talk over with me. I beg that you will not feel it necessary to disclose even the smallest hint of your purpose here. What I do not know, I cannot betray." A hint of mischief crept into her voice and an irrepressible dimple quivered as she added demurely, "I fear that one of Papa's favourite maxims was, 'Trust a woman with your money and your life, but never with a secret'."

Charles laughed, divided between relief and amusement. "Then I will take his advice," he accepted, smiling, "though indeed my immediate task is simply to be watchful. And in that you can help me if you will. You know these villages

158

and these people even better than I do myself, for I have been away too long. Look for anything that seems unusual — unexpected. But you must not seem to be watching. And if you should stumble on anything odd, however small it seems, don't on your life go enquiring into it, for that could be dangerous. Tell me of it straight away, or if it is quicker, tell Giles."

She thought this over carefully for a little while and then said with surprising shrewdness, "Something unusual — unexpected. Such as a fine town beau like my Uncle Nicholas making a prolonged stay in a village inn?"

"Yes. That kind of thing," agreed Charles, feeling rather uncomfortable. "Though in your uncle's case there seems to be a perfectly good reason for it."

She shrugged. "I do not believe he cares in the least about my behaviour or my reputation," she said calmly. "I think he has some plan to trick me out of my grandmother's money. But never mind my affairs. That *is* the kind of thing you mean?"

Charles nodded. "Exactly the kind of thing. But do, I beg of you, be careful. Simple as it seems, there really is danger. Grave danger."

She had promised to be careful, and no more was said on serious topics. They had returned reluctantly to the Fleece, and Giles had taken Galoon and Tina back to Springbourne, carrying Nell's promise that she would visit Emma later that afternoon.

Then Charles had disappeared. Where he had gone she had no notion, so was able to answer perfectly openly to Miss Smithson's enquiries about his whereabouts and plans, though indeed the poor woman only wished to know if he would be requiring a nuncheon. Nell herself was very glad to take a bowl of soup and some fruit after her spoilt breakfast and energetic morning. She chattered away freely about her afternoon plans, and Miss Smithson's reserve softened at the mention of Emma. She became positively human, and at last summoned up courage to ask diffidently if Miss Easton would be so obliging as to carry some of her curd tarts to Mistress

Woodstead, who had once commented favourably on their succulence.

Nell expressed her entire willingness to carry the gift and added her own appreciation of Miss Smithson's cookery. Miss Smithson flushed a dull and unbecoming pink and acknowledged that she was thought to have a light hand with pastries. Nell mentioned the hot milk, asking if she might have coffee or chocolate instead. But here she ran into unexpected opposition. Miss Smithson didn't exactly refuse. She simply said that milk was much safer, but it was abundantly clear from her attitude that Nell could expect to get milk. It was quite puzzling. Surely she didn't object to the small extra labour of making coffee or chocolate? And how was milk safer? More digestible perhaps? But as she had gone off to pack the curd tarts into a basket as soon as she had delivered her ultimatum, there was no opportunity for further argument.

Emma greeted her with loving warmth. It was quite difficult to believe, as she poured out the story of her adventures into those sympathetic ears, that only one day had elapsed since she had left the Lamb.

Emma listened and nodded and put in the odd word to encourage the flow of chatter, and when Nell reached the end of her story and handed over the basket of curd cakes she said, on a note of quiet satisfaction, "So you've made friends with Mag Smithson. That's good. She's a decent lass and an honest one, far different from her good-for-naught uncle. Why she stays with him is past my understanding, for I'm sure she could get a post with some respectable family. All she says is that he helped her when she was in need and that she'll stand by him. She's even stopped coming to Church. It's my belief the old skinflint keeps her so short of money she's none to put in the plate and is ashamed to come without."

"The poor thing!" exclaimed Nell indignantly. "Can't we do something to help her? He's a dreadful man. Charles says he's dangerous. We must get her away from him somehow."

Not by a flicker did Emma betray her amused pleasure at the easy use

162

of Charles's name and the implicit confidence in his judgements. Gravely she replied, "Time enough to be thinking of that when we get your affairs straightened out. Maybe you could take her into your service when you come to set up housekeeping, but dear knows when or where that will be. And she'll be a dour one to shift. Once she's made up her mind, she sticks to it."

Nell laughed. "I know. You should have heard her about the milk. You know how I hate it. I asked if I could have coffee or chocolate instead, but all she would say was that milk was safer — just as if I were a little baby girl. I know it'll be there waiting for me tonight. Ugh!"

Emma didn't answer immediately, so that Nell glanced up at her, to surprise an oddly measuring look directed at herself. There was a queer tense little silence, and then Emma said slowly, "You'll do well to take notice of what Mag Smithson says, Miss Nell. 'Tis no use pretending you're not in danger, for well we know you are. And if so be as anyone was wishful to do you a mischief, they could slip something in a cup of coffee so's maybe you'd go to sleep and never wake up again. Mag's right. Milk is safer. You'd be likely to taste anything queer about milk. Seems to me she knows or suspects more than she dare say, and she's doing her best to look after you."

Nell stared at her, eyes huge and dark in a little white face. It was one thing to speak lightly of a wicked uncle; quite another to face immediate and positive threat. "I s–see," she said slowly, and her voice sounded quavery and frightened in her own ears. She reacted promptly, bracing herself against the fear that had set her heart bumping. This shivering little coward was not her father's daughter. "I was just surprised," she explained in tacit apology. "We thought — Sir Charles and I — that I was safe enough for the time being, as Sir Nicholas would scarcely move against me openly."

"There's no telling what's in his mind, nor what needs are driving him," said Emma bluntly. "With such as him you can never be off your guard. Oh! If only I was up and about again and could see after you myself. To think of all the years that I've prayed for a son — and then this has to happen. I'll be out of this bed tomorrow, doctor or no doctor."

Nell realised that Emma considered the situation desperate indeed. Never before had she heard her rail against fate. Rather she had seemed to dispose of the fates of others. To hear her fretting at her own helplessness was rather as though the sun had suddenly decided to revolve in reverse. Nell did her best to offer reassurance and was reiterating a solemn promise to exercise the utmost caution when she was interrupted by sounds of arrival in the inn yard which drew her to the window in time to see Charles leap lightly down from a curricle, exchange a word or two with Giles who had gone to the heads of the splendid pair of greys which were harnessed to the light vehicle, and then stroll into the inn.

She turned back to the bed, her nervous qualms quite dispelled, exclaiming eagerly, "Sir Charles has just driven in, Emma, in *such* a turnout. Beautiful greys. Oh! Do you think he will invite me to drive back with him?"

The wish was to be granted. Bella came hastening in, face abeam, to ask if Mistress would receive Sir Charles, and the gentleman himself followed close on her heels. He was come, he explained, in the hope that Miss Easton would allow him to drive her back to the Fleece, and had ridden over to Trevannions especially to bring back the curricle. It was rather an antiquated vehicle, he added apologetically, since it had belonged to his father, but it would serve for the present.

"I really cannot have my betrothed wife trampling the countryside like a gypsy," he teased. "When you wish to visit Mistress Woodstead or your other friends in the neighbourhood, either Giles or I will drive you." Emma's eloquent grey gaze expressed the depth of her relief and gratitude.

Nell was thankful too, of course. It would be so very comfortable to have a stalwart defender always to hand. Yet the calm assumption of her submission to a check on her independence touched some irrational spring of resentment within her.

"Emma knows we're not really betrothed," she said, sounding, even in her own ears, like a cross child. "And you and Giles have better things to do than dancing attendance on me."

"But none more delightful," offered Charles gravely, quite unable to resist such an opening, and giving her his very best bow.

Nell coloured furiously though she knew he was only teasing, and was on the edge of impetuous retort when Emma intervened, saying sternly, "You'll do just as the Captain says, Miss Nell, and no nonsense. Whatever would your father say, to hear you arguing with your superior officer like that?"

This rather unusual method of controlling a rebellious nurseling silenced Nell and amused Charles, the latter registering a mental vow that his future offspring, if any, should be placed under military discipline from the moment of birth.

Emma was right in a way, conceded Nell reluctantly. Since she had consented to Charles's scheme and had engaged herself to help him, she supposed he did stand in the role of superior officer. A tactful enquiry as to whether she had ever driven a sporting carriage, coupled, upon her denial, with an offer to teach her how to handle the reins, was quite sufficient to dissipate any lingering traces of rebellion, and she danced downstairs eagerly to receive her first lesson. Since the greys had worked off the edge of their high spirits on the journey from Trevannions, she acquitted herself quite creditably, Charles, however, took over the reins as they neared the Fleece, feeling that his pupil could not yet be expected to negotiate the entrance to the stable yard. Indeed it exercised even his skill to manage the sharp turn from the lane through the narrow gate, and he had no attention to spare for what was happening in the yard, though he was vaguely aware that Nell's eager chatter had died away. Then, as the greys drew to a halt, he saw that the landlord was standing by the stable door, deep in converse with a stranger.

"Can you manage to get down without assistance?" he asked quietly, instinctively guessing how she would loathe the touch

168

of the man's hand. She slipped to the ground and was disappearing round the corner of the inn before the colloquy by the stable door had broken up, the newcomer springing forward to hold the horses. Charles, descending in more leisurely fashion, noted with interest that the greys, usually a fidgetty pair when not working, were standing quite quietly under the stranger's hands. Whoever he might be, he seemed to have a way with horses. But not, it would seem, with landlords. For Rudd was addressing him in reproving tones. "I tell you it's no use, man. Times are too hard. There's not work enough for the lad I've got, let alone another. Be off with you now."

Then he seemed to be overtaken by kindly inspiration, no doubt an unfamiliar visitor, since it caused him to clap a hand to his head in dramatic fashion and announce, with sudden and surprising fluency, "Unless the Captain here can maybe find a place for a chap as is handy with horses. Him being a military man might be willing to do a good turn for an old soldier that's fallen on hard times."

Charles surveyed the applicant for employment thoughtfully. He was of medium height and build, with a dark, hawklike, almost gypsyish cast of countenance, and looked to be about thirty years old.

"Old soldier are you? What regiment?"

"Eighteenth Dragoons, Sir. Ransome's my name, Tom Ransome."

"And your company commander?"

The man looked slightly disconcerted and hesitated perceptibly before he said with some reluctance, "Captain Little, Sir."

"Captain Little." Charles searched his memory. "No, I don't recall a Captain Little among my acquaintance. And what are you doing here? Were you discharged from the army?"

"After Corunna, Sir." The man was voluble now. "Lost the toes off me left foot with frost bite. Most of us 'ad no boots to our feet and the cold was something cruel. I was no use for soldiering after that. But I'm good with horses, Sir. Two beauties, these be," and he looked at Charles hopefully.

Charles was intrigued. "I might give

you a trial for a day or two," he said thoughtfully. "That would give me time to check your references. You have references, I suppose?"

The man nodded, and thrusting a hand into the recesses of a leather waistcoat which, in spite of the July heat, he wore over his coarse shirt, pulled out a paper which he handed over for Charles's perusal. It stated briefly that Sir John Blackadder of Hurstfield House in Norfolk was prepared to recommend Thomas Ransome for a place as groom or coachman, and to vouch for his sobriety and honesty.

It seemed to Charles that Ransome must value this testimonial very highly and care for it accordingly, for though it bore the date of October in the previous year, the paper was as fresh and uncreased as if it had been writ only yesterday; which Charles concluded that it probably had, and wondered if he might, by good luck or good management, be vouchsafed a glimpse of Sir Nicholas Easton's caligraphy. It would be interesting, he felt, to compare it with Sir John Blackadder's.

However he merely nodded, as one reasonably well satisfied, handed back the precious document, and said casually, "And I dare say Captain Little would speak for you?"

"Why yes, Sir, for sure he would," said Ransome without hesitation.

So whatever was planned for him was due to happen soon — before there could be any chance of his discovering whether Captain Little even existed. He controlled his mounting excitement and spoke lazily. "Very well. I'll give you a trial. You can stable the greys, and then Rudd will fix up quarters for you. I'll get in touch with Sir John Blackadder as soon as maybe."

"Yes, Sir," said his new groom with enthusiasm. "I think he'll speak well of me. And I'll do my best for you, Sir, I swear it."

Charles badly wanted to laugh. A paid assassin with a sense of humour! He could well imagine how the fellow would fulfil his promise. He nodded dismissal, and watched the impudent rogue lead the greys, now quite docile, stablewards. The man walked with a fluid catlike grace, treading in-toed, and with no hint of the expected limp. A gypsy horse coper, decided Charles, game for any kind of devil's work if the price was right. "Though I shouldn't have thought throat cutting was his line," he concluded critically, turning away to the inn door and devoting some attention to the possible means that might be used for his taking off.

He felt distinctly more cheerful at the prospect of action. This business of hanging about doing nothing was the very deuce. He whistled lightheartedly as he changed his attire for garments more suited to the dinner table. Dinner, with his enemies closing in for the kill, promised to be a stimulating meal.

12

CHARLES'S hopes of early action seemed doomed to disappointment. Day succeeded lovely summer day. Life pursued the gentle pattern of a pastoral idyll, with no hint of violence to mar its even tenor. It was just the kind of furlough that a soldier dreamed of — comfortable quarters and a delightful companion. Nell's total lack of the die-away airs of fashionable femininity, her frank candour, and the eager zest with which she greeted each day's adventure caused Charles to forget at times that she was not a boy. Together they visited the favourite haunts of his childhood. She listened in complete absorption to his stories of exploits which had seemed vastly exciting to a ten year old lad, ventured with him into the rather smelly cave which had been his favourite den, and gazed wistfully, with a sigh for hampering petticoats, at the tall tree which had been his lookout post and signal station. There were driving lessons and riding excursions to various beauty spots, and even one visit to Trevannions itself, where the housekeeper produced tea and plum cake and discoursed eagerly on domestic arrangements until Nell had thankfully made her escape to the stables to inspect a young colt foal.

In fact life was wholly idle and pleasant, and Charles was much inclined to cry out, as had a far more famous warrior, "Fie upon this quiet life! I want work."

Even Sir Nicholas seemed unusually tolerant and benign, raising no objection to the amount of time that his niece spent in Charles's society. He had not, as yet, had any reply to his enquiries about his brother's will. Indeed the Fleece was little disturbed by posts. Charles himself had not yet received a reply to the letter he had written to Sir John Blackadder. Since this had been entrusted to Sir Nicholas, who had kindly offered to carry it into Rye and hand it over to the mail coachman there in order to expedite its passage, he was not really surprised.

Whatever might be Charles's suspicions as to his character and purpose, Tom

Ransome was certainly a treasure as far as stable work was concerned. The greys bloomed under his attentions, their coats gleaming like wild silk, and their affection for him was so obvious that it actually gave Charles seriously to consider. Could a man be an out and out villain, a potential murderer, if he could so charm such sensitive and intelligent animals? Yet what other reason could there be for the very patent plot which had thrust Ransome into his orbit?

With Nell safely deposited with Emma, he had made cautious enquiries among certain old friends and acquaintances in the district. He had entirely failed to gather any information at all about Ransome. Bart Rudd was generally disliked, though no one could give adequate reasons. Charles was himself enough of a Sussex man to make due allowance for their innate distrust of 'furriners'. Enquiry about Sir Nicholas elicited little of value. One or two people, when pressed, awoke to the knowledge that he had been a surprisingly regular visitor to the district over the past four or five years, and admitted that they could think of no reason that should bring him about the place, unless it be the desire to re-stock a cellar depleted by the years of blockade. Further pursuit of this suggestion produced a negative reply from those who might be presumed to know, and the landlord of the Grape and Pigeon, where Charles was playing off the dust of an afternoon's futile enquiry, evoked an irreverent snort from his customer by suggesting that perhaps Sir Nicholas was 'one of these 'ere poetry writing coves' who needed country solitude for the composition of his works.

Nell was happy. In spite of the unresolved problems that clouded the future, she woke each day to the immediate sense of something delightful about to happen. She was perfectly well aware that this inner joy stemmed from the close comradeship that she shared with Charles, and disinclined to search her own heart any further. Better to take the present good and not worry too much about the future. After all, she once reminded herself, sipping resignedly at her bedtime milk, if Uncle Nicholas had his way, there might not be much future.

But thoughts of death and dissolution do not obsess the mind when one is seventeen years old and every day offers a delight previously unknown. The danger in which she dwelt came to mind occasionally. She was careful to lock her bedroom door, and once or twice she checked the priming of her pistol, assuring herself that all was in good order. The rest she left to Charles.

She had found a new hiding place for the pistol, in the pocket that Emma had put in her riding habit years before, when a couple of apples during a morning ride had been an essential barrier between herself and starvation. The pistol was rather a tight fit, but it was at least unlikely that anyone would go searching through her wardrobe for a concealed weapon, and as an added precaution she took care to hang the habit right at the back. It took a little time, extricating the pistol when she wanted to wear the habit, but it seemed safer than leaving it all the time in her workbag.

So matters rested for several days, halcyon days for Nell, while Charles concealed his anxieties and his mounting frustration as best he might. Once or twice he attempted to draw out Ransome in the hope of leading him into self betrayal, but Ransome, voluble enough over any matter concerning the horses, clammed up immediately when the talk turned to Peninsula reminiscences.

He approached Charles one sultry forenoon and asked if he might have some time off, as he wished to journey into Rye to make sundry small purchases and had found that he could get a ride in with the carrier's cart. As he gave careless consent, Charles wondered for a moment if it would be worth while trying to follow him, but Giles had gone over to Trevannions and would scarcely be back before evening, and he finally decided against going himself since it would leave Nell unguarded. Ransome assured him that young Jim would be on hand if the horses were needed before he got back, and shortly after noon could have been seen climbing into the much encumbered vehicle of his choice.

The afternoon was oppressively hot, seeming to presage a thunderstorm, and Nell was well content to retire to the orchard with her sewing. Before long Charles joined her, carrying a rug and an armful of cushions. They stood now upon such comfortable terms that he no longer asked her permission to sprawl his length beside her chair, while as to lighting one of his cigars — a habit that he had picked up in Spain and one that was frowned upon by polite society — she actually approved it, declaring that the smoke drove off the various winged beasties that infested the orchard, and that the aroma, out of doors, was unobjectionable. So the pair of them passed a comfortably lazy afternoon. Perhaps the lady's needlework did not make such rapid progress as it might have done, since much of her attention was diverted by the gentleman's idle converse which flitted from the Peninsula to London to Trevannions, with tales of the past and one or two vague dreams of the future, until it was time to think of changing one's dress for dinner, and where had the afternoon gone?

Nell gathered up her belongings and made her way back to the inn, leaving Charles to finish his cigar under the apple trees. She took out her fresh muslin and laid it on the bed with a fleeting thought of gratitude to Miss Smithson who had obviously spent some time in getting it up so beautifully. Of late the poor soul had seemed more than ever unhappy, hollow eyed and listless, her face frequently stained with signs of much weeping. But when Nell had gently tried to probe her grief she had evaded the questions and found some excuse to be off about her many duties.

Nell pondered the possibility that Emma had suggested of finding a place for her when she, Nell, should be established in a permanent home. For some unexplained reason this thought made her heart beat faster and brought a soft blush to her cheeks. She shook her head fiercely, determined to ignore these phenomena, bit back the little smile that had crept about her mouth, and crossed briskly to the wardrobe. Looking to the priming of her pistol would give her thoughts a more sensible direction. She took the tiny weapon from its snug concealment and carried it over to the broad window ledge where the light was better. The sky was darkening fast and already one or two long-drawn growls had heralded the approach of the storm that had threatened all day. Even as she laid the pistol down there was a brilliant flash of lightning, followed by a sharper crack. She was not nervous of storms, indeed rather enjoyed watching them. This one was still some distance away she judged, and opened her window, craning out to see if Charles was still in the orchard. She could just see his tall figure stooping to gather up the cushions. Doubtless the thunder had roused him to make good his retreat before the rain came.

As she stood watching, the stable door banged shut and Jim Cooke ran across the yard and into the kitchen. Charles had just made his way to the orchard gate when Jim came running out again and hurried down the path to meet him. She was too far away to hear what was said, but Jim appeared to be in a state of great excitement, and by the direction of his gestures something was amiss with the horses. Charles thrust his burden into the lad's arms and pushed him towards the house, then strode off rapidly in the direction of the stable.

Nell stood hesitating by the window for a moment, wondering whether she should go downstairs and find out what was wrong before she changed her dress. Her beloved Tina was stabled at Springbourne, but the big black Marquis and the greys were here at the Fleece. Giles, she knew, had ridden over to Trevannions on Galoon, taking Marshall, who had unaccountably loosened a shoe, to the farrier. Charles had disappeared inside the stable. It would be difficult to see in there, in the darkening brought by the storm. She could at least hold a lanthorn for him. And on this thought she was just turning away from the window when a movement in the yard caught her attention. Someone had just come into sight round the corner of the stable block and was approaching the door which Charles in his haste had left open. She recognized the supple loose-limbed gait so characteristic of Charles's new groom, and uttered a tiny gasp of relief that it was not Bart Rudd. But this relief was abruptly ended by Ransome's oddly furtive behaviour.

He was edging his way towards the open door without a sound, and from time to time he paused, obviously listening and glancing about him. There was something menacing about this stealthy approach. No honest groom, hurrying to his master's assistance, would behave so. Nell's heart began to beat in big uneven thumps and she suddenly found it difficult to breathe. Ransome had reached the stable door and now slid round it, out of her sight. Without further hesitation she climbed on to the window ledge, caught up her pistol, and let herself drop to the mounting block below. There was a sharp ripping noise as her skirt caught on the window latch. She wrenched it free, sprang down the rough stone steps, and ran on light slippered feet across the yard. Instinct bade her make her entry with due caution. Hardly knowing what to expect she slipped round the open door, trying to control her hurried breathing.

But there was quite enough noise within to mask any sound she might have made. Nor was the stable in the semi-darkness she had expected. Someone had lit a lanthorn which was hanging on a hook on the far wall and it cast on floor and walls the weird distorted shadows of a frantic horse. In the first two stalls the greys were standing fairly quietly except for a little nervous tossing and stamping. Then came several empty stalls and one which housed the landlord's phlegmatic cob, all of them in shadow made deeper by the circle of light from the lantern which fell on the loose box at the far end where Marquis was trampling, rearing, shaking his head wildly and uttering high piercing squeals, though whether of rage or terror it was impossible to decide. Whatever the cause it would certainly be courting death to enter the box with that raging power loose inside it. Charles, she could see, was not attempting it. With his back to her he was leaning on the half-door talking to the horse in a low soothing voice, but as yet the effect was negligible. Of Ransome there was no sign.

Nell stood perfectly still. She had seen him enter the stable, and since there was no other exit save to the hayloft above, he must be hidden in one of the empty stalls. Deliberately she set herself to breathe slowly and evenly, eyes and ears alert for the first sign of movement, pistol steady in her hand. From this point of vantage she could keep Charles covered, and that was far more sensible than running to him as she longed to do, to pour out some incoherent warning of a danger only half comprehended. But the waiting seemed endless, as Charles went on talking to the horse and she stood with every sense keyed and straining.

Presently Charles shifted his position slightly, and almost immediately the shadowy form of Ransome appeared in the mouth of one of the stalls at the far end. Only a moment he paused, and she saw that he was grasping a short thick cudgel. Then swift, silent, he was leaping towards Charles, cudgel arm whirling up to strike as he sprang. For Nell everything seemed to happen at once. Afterwards she could never remember firing but only that she had thought, I mustn't kill him, just disable him, for what could we do with a dead body? It never occurred to her that in that murky shadow-blotched light she might miss altogether and perhaps hit Charles instead, and this, she declared, was fortunate since the thought would certainly have spoiled her aim. As it was, her whole being was concentrated on the upraised arm that held the cudgel.

As she fired, Charles seemed suddenly to become aware of his assailant and swung round in one smooth powerful sweep, his left fist coming over to catch the groom a heavy blow on the temple which dropped him in a limp heap on the floor. Then he stared incredulously at the slim little creature in the shadows.

"Nell! What the devil? I thought 'twas our dear friend Rudd or your loving uncle shooting at me!"

She tried to smile at him, though rather shakily, and reached out to lay the pistol on a convenient shelf with fingers now a little tremulous.

"No. Just me," she said in a funny little husk of a voice that quivered between tears and laughter. And then, more anxiously, "I haven't killed him have I?"

Charles grinned. "You're much too good a shot for that, my child. Dead on target I suspect. Through the fleshy part of his forearm. Wasn't that what you intended?"

But Nell was still too shaken to respond in equally light-hearted vein. "Then why does he lie so still?" she asked doubtfully.

"Ah! That's my handiwork. He should sleep peacefully for quite some time. Meanwhile I'll tie him up snugly and dump him in the loft." He jerked his head at the trap door which gave access to it, just above them.

"And you're sure he'll be all right?" insisted Nell, with feminine inconsistency.

"Quite as well as is necessary," said Charles grimly. "The gentleman has a few questions to answer before I concern myself unduly with his comfort. Help me now, will you, Nell? There's no time to lose. With any luck they'll take your shot for another crack of thunder, and we'll have him safely tucked away and no one the wiser. A bandage to stop this bleeding first — not that he deserves any particular consideration, but we can't have him bleeding all over the floor and betraying us."

This callous attitude had the intended effect of steadying Nell, so that she was able to assist in the task of binding

188

Charles's handkerchief over an ugly looking wound with comparative fortitude in spite of her lack of experience. After that she was dispatched to bring a couple of spare halters and some leather straps, while Charles hauled the unconscious groom to the foot of the ladder, hoisted him over his shoulder, and managed to climb far enough up to slide his burden through the open trap, after which he climbed over him and dragged him to the far corner of the loft. So much accomplished, it took only a few minutes to ensure that he was securely bound and that the hay was so disposed about him as to conceal his presence from any cursory inspection. He had just completed this to his satisfaction when a voice from the region of his ankles enquired, "Did you gag him? Because if you didn't, and he recovers consciousness and calls for help, we shall have had all this trouble for nothing," and turning, he saw Nell's head and shoulders projecting through the trap in most unladylike fashion.

He bit back a strong inclination to laugh. This was no comedy, and in spite of her brave words he guessed that she was more anxious than she was willing to admit. "There's just the one difficulty," he explained. "No gag. I used my handkerchief on his arm and yours is much too small."

Nell promptly suggested using a strip of fabric from the skirt of her dress. "It's ruined already," she said, her voice echoing oddly as she retired down the ladder, "I tore it climbing out of the window. Here you are," and she tossed up an ample length of material rolled up into a ball.

Charles adjusted the gag carefully, since he had no wish to suffocate the captive, and then followed her down the ladder. He cast a quick glance over the scene of the recent operations and stooped to pick up the cudgel which had fallen from Ransome's hand. There was a metallic clang as he lifted it, and Nell turned curiously, to see him frowning thoughtfully at a piece of a horse shoe which had been nailed to the wood.

"I see," he said softly. "Very neat. Tragic accident. Officer dies after being kicked by his own horse. I don't suppose you thought that one out for yourself,

Master Ransome. Well — perhaps you'll not meddle with my horses again. I wonder what you gave this poor old fellow," and he turned to look at Marquis, now standing quiet, even dejected, head a-droop after his wild display of temperament, and then went quietly into the loose box and ran a knowledgeable hand over the horse's neck and withers. "Not much amiss with you now, is there? Come to think of it I've a notion he'd hate to do you any real damage, whatever he did to your master."

Nell, who had been examining the deadly cudgel with fascinated horror, now said, "Wasn't it the storm that upset him then? I've known horses terrified like that by thunder and lightning."

"That's what we were meant to think. But they don't know Marquis. Neither thunder nor gunfire ever disturb him. Steady as a rock. And he's gone through storms in Spain that make this one sound like a spring shower."

As though to refute this rash statement there was another crash of thunder, followed almost immediately by the steady drumming of rain on the stable roof.

"We must get back to the house," Charles went on. "Can you manage to forget all that has happened in this last quarter of an hour?"

"I'll try," she said dubiously. "But I hope Sir Nicholas doesn't ask what we've been doing. I should blush or stammer, I know."

"Nonsense," declared Charles hearteningly, "you'll be as cool and steady as you were just now. And I'd not wish for a better comrade in emergency."

At this high praise Nell did indeed blush furiously, and to cover her confusion made a great business of picking up the pistol and moving towards the door. "You're quite sure he'll be all right?" she asked again, glancing up at the, trap door. "I mean — I don't want him to die or anything."

"No need to fret for *him*," said Charles unsympathetically. "He'll be worse before I'm through with him. Now — can you manage to climb in through your window again? For you're in no case to meet inquisitive eyes."

Nell glanced down at her dress. Apart from a long rent which ran from high waist to ruffled hem and permitted a snowy petticoat to foam out rather enticingly, she had completed the wreckage by kneeling on the stable floor, thereby acquiring sundry mud and bloodstains.

"Oh dear!" she said ruefully. "What will Miss Smithson think? I'll have to hide it until I've time to think up a credible story. This is one time when I *couldn't* tell the truth." She turned to leave the stable, adding shyly, "Do you think you could help me up to the window? I don't think I can manage on my own without a ladder. I'm not very heavy."

"After heaving Ransome around, I should think I could toss you up with one hand," he replied cheerfully.

In the event it took two, to lift her until she was able to scramble in over the window sill, with, alas, a most improper display of slim ankles, of which Charles, even in his preoccupation, was not unappreciative.

13

IN spite of the frantic haste with which their respective toilets had been performed, both lady and gentleman appeared perfectly elegant and point-de-vice when they met again over the dinner table. Nell had been conscious of a fast beating heart and a certain dryness in the mouth as she had come into the dining-room prepared to face her uncle. He was not there. And when Charles joined her a minute or two later, Rudd had come in to ask whether he should serve their dinner at once, or whether they would wait for Sir Nicholas. His niece, he explained, was fretting for fear the cutlets would be scorched. No, in reply to Charles's query, Sir Nicholas was not yet come in. No doubt he had taken shelter somewhere to wait for the storm to pass.

They decided not to wait for him and sat down to dinner, but it was, of course, impossible to discuss the subject that was uppermost in both their minds while they were being served. They talked spasmodically on various innocuous topics, with Charles bearing the greater share of the conversational burden and Nell a little inclined to fall into abstracted silence. She came to life eagerly enough when the covers were finally drawn and it seemed safe to assume that the landlord would now be fully occupied in the taproom. "Now," she breathed urgently, "tell me what you are going to do with him, and why did he attack you like that? Quickly, before Sir Nicholas comes back."

"Not so fast," reproved Charles. "First we must set the scene a little. It won't do to be found deep in talk which breaks off abruptly on Sir Nicholas's entry. He would be bound to suspect us, and it is my object, should he return, to puzzle him a little by appearing completely ignorant of any untoward happening. I think — yes — we shall have had a lovers' tiff. You should occupy yourself with your sewing, and I shall play patience." He began to lay out the cards. "Though I do not expect his early return. He will allow ample opportunity for the shocking discovery to be made first."

"Then you think" — obediently she was unfolding her needlework — "that he is behind this attempt on your life?"

"Sure of it. But being sure isn't proof."

"But why? What grudge can he have against you?"

Charles shrugged. "I can think of several. Certainly I am a hindrance to his plans for you. But no matter for his reasons. The thing is to bring the attempt home to him. Even if I can get an admission out of Ransome, it will serve us little. No court of law is going to listen to his allegations against a man of Sir Nicholas's standing. And Sir Nicholas, you perceive, is not even here. Doubtless he is several miles away, with, I daresay, any number of perfectly respectable people to vouch for his whereabouts. As things stand we can do nothing. But I may be able to pick up some hint from Ransome that will enable me to set a trap of my own."

"Do you think Rudd is in the plot too?"

196

"In league with your uncle and Ransome — yes. Aware of this particular attempt, I think not. I was observing him closely and could see no hint of surprise or disappointment in his face when I walked in perfectly sound and well. No doubt it seemed good to Sir Nicholas to leave him in ignorance of the actual plan. He's no actor, and might play his part better if it were spontaneous. I should think, having been foiled at the first attempt, they will wait a little before trying again."

Nell looked doubtful and anxious. "Emma says there's no knowing what necessities are driving my uncle. Please be careful. I could not bear it if anything were to happen to you because of me."

Charles reassured her as best he could, promising extreme watchfulness and expounding cheerfully on the general superiority of one Light Bob to any number of clumsy plotters. She smiled dutifully in response to his rallying tones but was not comforted. It seemed to her that the plot had been far from clumsy and had come dangerously close to success. But her anxieties could not help Charles, so she did her best to conceal them. When, however, he suggested that he had better proceed with his interrogation of the prisoner before anyone set up a hue and cry over his disappearance, her courage wavered a little, and she asked if she could go with him, not from any wish to be present at the interview but because she did not relish the prospect of being left alone to face Sir Nicholas.

Charles shook his head. "It might be necessary for you to cover my absence," he said, and did not add that it might also be necessary to use methods of extracting information that would be quite unsuitable to a lady's sensibilities. "I plan to carry Ransome over to Trevannions as soon as Giles is back," he went on. "Rascal though he is, we shall have to dig your bullet out of him, and it can scarcely be done here. At Trevannions I can hold him safe. We cannot let him go scot free, but I have no time now to devise his ultimate fate. Now pay heed, Nell, for this is of vital importance. I may well be gone all night, for we must first find a suitable vehicle in which to transport our prisoner. I can scarcely drive about the country-side in a curricle, displaying him to anyone who might be interested. While I am away, trust no one. See that your pistol is ready to hand and keep your bedroom door locked. And that window — far too easy of access. Closed, please, and the shutters too. Above all," he emphasised, "go nowhere alone with your uncle or Rudd. Feign a headache and keep your room. Is it understood?"

She nodded, looking up at him, wan-faced but trustful.

"Good girl. I think you *must* be safe for this evening. Sir Nicholas will surely wait to ascertain my fate, and if Ransome and I are both missing, that will pose him a pretty problem. And I promise you that either Giles or I will be back as soon as is possible."

He smiled down at her — the smile she was learning to look for — the corners of his mouth indrawn as though he was reluctant to let the smile have full play, the firm lips curving and softening in a way that aroused certain reprehensible longings in her girlish heart. "And I have never thanked you for coming to my aid in the stable," he went on, considering the matter thoughtfully for a moment and then saying the thing he knew would please her best. "Your father would have been so very proud."

She looked down shyly, pleased but embarrassed by his praise. He held out his hand, and after a momentary surprised hesitation she put hers into it. Her slim cool fingers showed pale against his brown fist, and on a sudden impulse he raised the small hand to his lips and lightly kissed it. It quivered for a moment in his clasp and then was gently withdrawn.

What in all creation had made him do that? He had never, in all his life, kissed a woman's hand or even wished to do so. It was his turn to feel shy and awkward, not sure whether to be glad or sorry that there was no time for more of this rather pleasant dalliance. It would have been easy to yield to a strong temptation to turn the confiding little hand in his and set his lips to soft palm and delicate wrist.

His leave taking was abrupt almost

to curtness, but Nell did not notice. Left alone, she very gently raised the hand that he had kissed and held it against her cheek, savouring again the blissful moment when his warm mouth had caressed it. Sewing abandoned in her lap, she sat dreaming of even more rapturous possibilities. Nor did she rouse from her happy reverie until the door opened quietly and Sir Nicholas strolled into the room.

"Why, my dear," he said on a note of gentle surprise. "All alone? What has become of your devoted suitor?"

Charles had asked her to cover up for him, and she had wasted the time in idle dreaming. Frantically her mind sought for some plausible tale. Sir Nicholas was watching her, bright-eyed, expectant. Then, blessedly, inspiration came with the memory of Charles's laughing remark about a lovers' tiff. She tossed her head slightly and did her best to look affronted. "I'm sure I don't know." She did her best to make it sound petulant rather than merely sulky. "Did you wish to speak with him, sir? For if so, I will retire. I have the headache a little."

Sir Nicholas's brows twitched together. It was difficult to remain quite unmoved at this crisis in his affairs. With his plans so delicately balanced a quarrel between his niece and her betrothed was the last thing he wanted just now. It would sort ill with the pathetic picture of a lovelorn maiden driven to self destruction. He disclaimed any especial desire to talk with Charles, sympathised with his niece's headache, which he unhesitatingly ascribed to the thunderstorm, and graciously pressed her to try one of the cachets which he himself used to alleviate the occasional headaches brought on by over application.

With a memory of Emma's warning ringing in her ears, Nell's refusal was more curt than courteous. Her headache, she said, would be better by morning, and she never took strange medicines.

"Ah you young people!" smiled Sir Nicholas, still gracious. "What a wonderful thing it is to have such powers of recuperation. And I am sure you are quite right, my dear, not to be for ever quacking yourself. But these cachets of mine are not just in the common way. They are made especially for me by a friend who is a very learned physician. If your headache is not better by morning, I shall certainly insist upon your trying one," and he wagged a finger at her playfully.

She made no further protest, though she had no intention of submitting to the promised medication. She would have liked to plead the headache as an excuse to withdraw to her room, but she could not be sure that sufficient time had elapsed to allow the two men to get clear away with their prisoner, and she dare not leave Sir Nicholas free to go in search of them. She busied herself in sorting out some tangled silks, and began to ply her uncle with questions about her aunt and cousin and life in London, hoping that this sudden interest didn't sound as forced and artificial in his ears as it did in hers.

The evening dragged its interminable length, and it was with difficulty that she restrained a sigh of relief when the clock at last struck ten. Surely by now it must be safe to relax her painstaking efforts. Thankfully she laid aside her work and bade her uncle a polite good night.

Her small room felt like a haven of refuge after the strain of the evening. She locked the door as she had been bidden, and carefully cleaned and reloaded the pistol, discovering a new and delicious excitement in the thought that she was submitting to Charles's commands. To be sure the room would be dreadfully stuffy with the window closed, but he had said that she must close it, and obedience to his will was her present delight. She leaned out of the window for a moment, sniffing the delicious smell of the rain cooled earth. There was no gleam of light from the stable block. She must be patient and wait till morning to hear the final outcome of the affair. She closed and latched the casement and unfolded the heavy shutters from their recesses in the walls, drawing them across the window and swinging into place the heavy bar that locked them into position. The room was beginning to look like a beleaguered fortress. She only hoped that the inn didn't catch fire during the night, for barricaded as she was it seemed highly probable that she would perish in the flames before help could reach her.

14

GILES snipped the last length of sticking plaster and dropped the roll on to the table which already held a motley collection of bowls, swabs, probes and forceps. The man on the bed scowled up at him without gratitude.

"He'll do now," announced the self-appointed surgeon. "Luck of the devil's own — naught but torn flesh, as'll heal easy enough. Born to be hanged, that's you," he apostrophised the patient, "and the sooner the better."

"Yes, well, we'll see about that, all in good time." Charles sounded rather amused by his henchman's venom. "Now if we just secure that arm to his body" — and he proceeded to wind the injured groom into a helpless cocoon with broad strips of torn sheet, which was probably good for the immobilisation of the wounded limb but certainly put a premium on any attempt at escape, after which he picked up a cup from the table where Giles had dropped the sticking plaster.

"Just lift him up so that he can drink," he said, "and then you can be getting back. I'll manage well enough now, and I don't want — the place — " he hurriedly substituted, "left unguarded."

Obediently, though without any significant gentleness, Giles hauled his patient into a semi-recumbent position and thrust a couple of spare pillows behind him.

"I want naught of your drinks," the man snarled at him, and spat a foul oath.

"Nor I wouldn't be wasting good brandy on scum the likes of you," retorted Giles, "but orders is orders, and if the Captain says drink, you drinks, see?" And taking the cup from Charles's hand, he forced the rim between the man's clenched teeth and tilted it so that the liquid ran down his gullet. The unwilling recipient choked, gulped and then swallowed, with diminished reluctance as he realized that he was indeed drinking brandy and water.

The cup drained, he was permitted to lie back against the pillow, and Charles had the satisfaction of seeing his sickly pallor yield to a more normal colour. Having assured himself that the bonds securing the prisoner to the bed frame were still intact, and taken the further precaution of removing the lamp from it's position by the bed and placing it well out of reach on the mantel shelf, he followed Giles out of the room, assuring the prisoner that he would shortly return to talk with him, and would not keep him waiting long.

He was as good as his word. He and Giles had already agreed that the big groom should show no concern over the absence of his master, or of Ransome, who was after all only a chance-come gypsy. Sir Charles would no doubt turn up in his own good time, and Ransome was little loss.

"Keep your eyes and ears open, but don't try to follow them. And take good care of Miss Nell."

Giles grinned and shook his head. "Seems like as if the boot's on the other foot," he suggested slyly. "She do seem to have taken good care of thee Master Charles. 'Twarn't your bullet I dug out of that rapscallion. Eh! She's a mettlesome lass, and a real credit to the regiment." And off he went, chuckling to himself at the way at which he had scored off his master, and apparently as fresh as though he had not ridden or driven some forty miles, helped to smuggle an unconscious man from the Fleece to Trevannions, and topped off with a gory surgical operation.

Charles returned to the old nursery, which had been considered the most suitable place for the bestowal of the captive, since it's windows were barred and it was situated at a distance from the inhabited portion of the house.

Ransome's features were set in a mask of determined obstinancy. He was clearly commiting himself to a course of dumb resistance. If he simply refused to utter he could neither betray his masters nor further incriminate himself.

Charles drew up a chair to the side of the bed, poured himself a glass of brandy from the decanter which still stood on the cluttered table, and eyed his subject thoughtfully. There was something hearteningly familiar about the set of Ransome's mouth. Not for nothing had Charles served his term as an efficient and well liked company officer. A man in that mood would undergo the tortures of the damned rather than utter one word that might reveal his secrets. Possibly the brandy had been a mistake. But Giles's surgery, while not deliberately brutal, had been rather rough and ready, and the poor devil had endured without so much as a grunt.

Such a man was unlikely to break. But in Charles's experience he might well, if unfairly accused of something not directly connected with his secret, defend himself with the utmost volubility. Sometimes in this relaxed mood he could be led to reveal what was required. The essential thing was to get him talking. With a pretty fair notion of the fellow's one soft spot, he was prompt to attack.

"How dare you meddle with my horse?" he said in a voice of cold fury, and saw at once that he had scored a hit. The man's eyes flickered in surprise and the set lips parted slightly.

"Thanks to you," Charles ranted on, "I've had to call in the farrier to destroy an animal that's worth a dozen of your worthless carcase. What witches brew did you give him?"

"I didn't — you can't — there's no call to have him destroyed," the man stammered, his face alive with genuine concern. "I'd not harm any horse — least of all a grand fellow like the Marquis. You leave him be. He'll take no hurt from aught I gave him."

"And I suppose I'd have taken no hurt from what you tried to give me?" retorted Charles.

Ransome showed signs of relapsing into the sullens once more.

"I suppose you never stopped to think that if you succeeded in finishing me, the Marquis would have been blamed, and would certainly have been destroyed as vicious?"

"They wouldn't never? A valuable animal like that? Why if I'd known that I never would have taken the job on. But it seemed an easy way of — " He broke off, realizing that he was being led into indiscretion, and scowled angrily at Charles.

"Yes. Why did you take it on? What

was your grudge against me, that you were so anxious to put a period to my existence?" enquired Charles lazily, as one only mildly interested.

"You're a military man, and I hates 'em all. And with good cause, Mister Captain," growled Ransome. "*He* was a Captain, too. Now if I could only get a chance at him, I'd not use a bit of a stick. Just to get my two 'ands round 'is throat and squeeze and squeeze, gentle like, so's it took a nice long time, and 'im knowing it was me, and paying at last for all 'e done to us."

He was talking freely enough now, if rather incoherently, his face flushed and his eyes glittering oddly. Charles realised that he was becoming feverish, but this was no time to develop scruples over listening to his ramblings. If, by so doing, he could get the information that he sought, he would not cavil at the means. He poured a little brandy into the cup and filled it up with cold water. "Thirsty?" he asked. And at Ransome's nod held the cup to his lips. "Don't think me grudging of the brandy now," he said carelessly. "Your wound's nothing so desperate, but I've seen enough of such to know that too much wine only inflames them."

He set the cup down. "Tell me about the captain you wanted to choke the life out of," he invited.

"Aye. Him — and his father, and his dear kind lady mother," jerked the man viciously. "And my own precious master that was mild and sweet as mare's milk because they was gentry born and he was new-come-up, with his, 'Why, yes indeed, Sir Gerald,' and, 'I'm sure you're in the right of it, Lady Maria,'" — he mimicked the genteel accents with biting precision — "and the whole lot of them as cold and hard-hearted as Judas Iscariot himself."

Some sharpening of his blurred and fevered gaze caught the momentary surprise in Charles's expression, and read it aright. "Thought I was an ignorant heathen gypsy as 'ad never 'eard of such, didn't you?" he jeered, and sank back wearily on to the pillows. For a little while he lay with closed eyes, the harsh lines of his face slowly relaxing, and when he again took up his tale he

212

spoke more quietly. "And so I would have been if it hadn't been for my Meg. She was like a gentle angel was Meg. She loved me true, poor and rough as I was, and she tried to teach me about what was right, just as her mother had taught her. Put her into service with Sir Gerald and Lady Maria, her mother had, just before she died of the lung rot. Thought her daughter'd be safe for ever in good service. Safe!" The voice was savagely bitter. "Well — I reckon she thought 'twas best, poor soul, Meg's father being dead, and her uncle — well you know what *he* is. She'd no one else to turn to, and her dying."

Delirious, thought Charles, for what part could *he* have in this rambling tale, and how should he know anything about this mysterious uncle?

Ransome's eyes were half closed now, but the hoarse voice took up its burden once more. "We were promised, Meg and me. I was only under groom, but I'd always a knack with the horses. We made it up as we'd be wed as soon as I got to be groom, for there was snug quarters over the stables that we could have, and we was happy, planning and saving. And then young Master Gerald comes home. *Captain* Gerald I should say. And with naught better to amuse himself, he sets to seducing my Meg, though we two silly greenheads never guessed what he was at. It was her job, seeing as she was upstairs maid, to see to his room and his linen, and he was for ever a ringing for her and wanting this and that. Real pleasant he seemed, and often slipped her a shilling, which we was both pleased about, seeing it helped on our savings."

He fell silent again. Charles watched him quietly, touched by pity even for his would-be murderer, for truth and tragedy grated through every bitter syllable, and it was only too easy to guess what was coming.

"Drunk, he was, the night it happened," the tired voice broke across his reflections, "though she didn't guess it at first when he sent for her. And when she knew what he would be at, she fought him as best she could. But she darsn't cry out, for well she knew who'd be blamed. So he forced her. She came crying to me in the wood next night — a pretty place it was, where we used to meet times, with the bluebells and the wild bracken, and told me 'twas all over between us, for she was no maid any more and not fitting for me to marry. Wild, she talked, about throwing herself in the river and ending her shame. By and by I got her quieted down a bit, and she promised she'd not do anything 'thout telling me, and when I left her she seemed more sensible like."

"Going back through the wood I was planning on going to the master and asking if he'd let us have a little place, so's we could be married and I could look after her. That was when I comes across this rabbit. 'Twas caught in one of they spring traps. Any other time I'd have knocked it on the head and left it, for what would I want with a rabbit, getting my victuals regular enough? But that night — well — there was a look in its eyes that made me think of Meg, and when I touched it, its fur was soft like her hair. I forced the trap open with a bit of a branch and lifted it out, and it was while I was stood with it in my hands, looking at its crushed leg and thinking I'd best put it out of its misery after all, that they took me."

He lay quietly for a while and the drooping eyelids closed. Charles thought he was drowsing off — a pity — for so far the rambling talk had revealed nothing of value and had only served to arouse his sympathy for the fellow. But in a moment or two the head on the pillow stirred restlessly, the heavy eyes opened again, and a smile of purest satisfaction curved the tired mouth.

"I can't never be truly sorry for it — though I know 'twas because of that everything went wrong. 'Twasn't so much the keeper you see — a decent enough lad as'd never have split on me for one rabbit, even if I 'ad took it — but just as I was a'going to tell 'im and show 'im the trap, who should come strolling up but our young master Captain Gerald. And when I saw 'is smooth smirking face — I let 'im 'ave it. The thought of 'im and my Meg — "

Even at the memory his left hand — the good one — bunched itself into a powerful fist, and Charles could see the ripple of the muscles in the forearm and the lift in the shoulder. It had been a mighty, a soul satisfying blow, which had deprived the dis-Honourable Gerald of two front teeth and spread his aristocratic nose over his dissipated countenance in such fashion that it was never quite the same again.

But it had been a solitary satisfaction and a costly one. The keeper — up to that point a friendly neutral — had felt bound to come to the aid of his employer's son, and not being handy with his fists had used the butt of his gun. Young Ransome had come to himself in the lock-up. Characteristically he had taken refuge in stubborn silence, determined not to involve Meg in his troubles, and had steadfastly refused to give any explanation which might have mitigated his crime. So it was not surprising that he had been sentenced to transportation, having been found guilty of the heinous crime of poaching, seriously aggravated, of course, by his dastardly attack on an innocent young man. Fortunate to escape hanging, he was severely informed.

He had served several years of his sentence under appalling, brutalising conditions, before an opportunity of escape occurred and he was able to make his way back to England. Since he had neither friends nor money it seemed probable that this had been achieved by a combination of cunning and violence, but he volunteered no details. His search for Meg had done nothing to dissipate the bitter rancour with which he was consumed. His enquiries — necessarily furtive, since his very presence in the country must be concealed — had discovered the fact that she had been summarily dismissed from her post upon the realisation that she was pregnant, and that he himself was generally held to be responsible for her condition.

It had taken him another six months to trace her, and then only through a chance meeting with a lad who had given her a lift in his cart when she was turned away from the manor. He had felt sorry for the poor lass, and had set her several miles on her way. She was going, she told him, to seek her uncle, the only relative she had. Ransome had known vaguely of the uncle's existence but since Meg had always spoken of him with fear and dislike had never dreamed that she would seek refuge with him. It had been fairly simple after that to trace her to the village of Wintringham. "The brat," he said, "was dead — born dead." And his Meg still drudged for her brute of an uncle because he had taken her in when her need was desperate.

Charles gasped, and stared at him. Not till that moment had he identified the meek, much harassed Miss Smithson with the pathetic little heroine of Ransome's story. The silence lengthened. His story done, Ransome seemed to be yielding to exhaustion, his eyes closed, a pallid shade about his mouth.

"I still don't see why you tried to murder me," Charles objected. "Hadn't you troubles enough? You say yourself that you're lying low. This afternoon's little caper was just the thing to draw attention on yourself. As my groom you would certainly have been required to give evidence. Why didn't you just take your Meg and make off with her?"

The heavy lids were raised, and the dark eyes regarded him steadily with a touch of weary scorn. "Aye. You would think like that. You well-breeched swells that's never had to worry where the ready's coming from. A chap on his own can manage somehow. There's ways and means of getting about for one who ain't too particular. But my Meg's a decent woman. I'll not have her mixed up with such company. So how was I to get her out of the country — and where could we go — without money? I was offered a fair price for the job and I took it, see? I don't say I liked it. You wasn't a bad sort of a cove, and you'd a good eye for a horse, and murder's a dirty business. But it was a chance to bring the pair of us off — and I took it."

"And I suppose Sir Nicholas threatened to inform against you if you didn't," said Charles gently. "Tell me, what's my price? I'm eager to know what value he sets on me."

The dark eyes widened, and the man struggled to raise himself on his sound elbow, glaring at Charles with a recurrence of his old hostility. "Who said 'twas Sir Nicholas?" he demanded fiercely. "I never did, no, nor I wouldn't tell you who paid me, whatever you done."

Charles pressed him back on the pillow. "Lie still, or you'll start that arm bleeding again. And content yourself. You gave nothing away. There was no need. I've known what your purpose was ever since Rudd first brought you to my notice."

"And still took me on? You're a mighty cool hand, Governor, ain't you?"

Charles laughed. "I'll admit to certain qualms," he acknowledged. "But I judged you were not addicted to throat slitting, and shooting seemed unlikely if my death was to be disguised as accident, as seemed most probable. After all another mysterious murder in the same locality might call for more ingenuity of explanation than even Sir Nicholas could well supply."

It was obvious that this was news to the prisoner. "Another murder?" he asked.

"Why yes. A young man was found with his throat cut, a month or two back — a young man who had been staying at the Fleece. Did not your amiable fellow conspirators advise you of this? Or tell you that, the victim being heir to an earldom, the matter was by no means forgotten?"

"They never told me about no young man being murdered," Ransome muttered sullenly. "Meg did warn me not to have anything to do with their schemes. Up to no good, she said, the pair of them. So I didn't tell her about the job I was to do. They said you was a spy, nosing out all you could about the trade in these parts. Now me, I've good cause to be grateful to the Gentlemen, and I don't like spies. So what with one thing and another — " He shrugged, winced, and fell silent again.

Charles, too, was deep in thought. He seemed to have made little progress unless it could be counted as progress to have Ransome's confirmation that Sir Nicholas and Rudd were in league together, and that, after all, had been pretty evident from the start. He decided to leave further decision till morning, or rather till he had slept on it, a glance at the clock assuring him that morning had already come. Better snatch some sleep while he could. He got up, yawning, and picked up the lamp.

"I'll leave you to sleep," he said casually and strolled over to the door. A voice from the bed arrested him as his hand went to the latch.

"Sir!" For the first time it was urgent and appealing. He looked back. Ransome had flung over towards him as far as his bonds would permit. Charles felt again that illogical touch of pity. "Sir!" the hoarse voice repeated, gulping now in it's desperate pleading, "I know you owes me nothing — though I swear I never harmed the Marquis — but, Sir, don't let Meg know! She's had enough to bear. If she knows I went to my death just through coming back for her, it'll just about finish her. If you just don't say nothing, maybe she'll never find out how I ended." His eyes were fixed hungrily on Charles's face, not daring to hope, just waiting.

Charles nodded curtly. "I'll do what I can," he said, and went out, locking the door behind him.

15

PERHAPS it was the unusual circumstances of the closed and shuttered window that caused Nell to sleep late next morning. It was the clatter of a pail, knocked over or dropped on the cobblestones that finally aroused her to a room that was, of course, in darkness, only the thin line of light where the shutters met confirming the idea that it must be day.

She slipped out of bed, pulled on her dressing gown, and went across to open the shutters, fumbling with the unfamiliar button that fastened the bar and pinching a careless fingertip in the hinge, but managing eventually to fold them back into place. A cautious peep through the window assured her that there was no one about. What should she do? Charles had bidden her keep her room, but if she did that, how was she to discover what was happening? She stood thoughtfully sucking the injured finger and decided on compromise. Walking over to the hearth she pulled the bell, then unlocked the door and scrambled back into bed again.

It was some little time before the summons was answered, and she was beginning to wonder if the bell was out of order when the expected knock sounded on the door panel and Miss Smithson came into the room. Nell glanced up at her, a request to be given breakfast in bed hovering on her lips, and uttered instead a startled exclamation of shocked pity. The woman looked almost distraught. Her normally pale face was sheet white, except where a blue bruise disfigured one cheek. There were olive purple smudges under her eyes, eyes that were dully glazed beneath their swollen lids. Even her prim cap was set awry for once, permitting strands of soft brown hair to straggle untidily about her face. But it was the way in which her lips were twisting and working, as though they were forming words that she dare not utter, that really tore at Nell's heart.

With no thought for anything save to offer comfort, she jumped out of bed and ran to catch the cold shaking fingers in her own warm young hands. "You poor dear," she said gently. "Come and sit down and tell me what has happened. What have you done to your cheek?" And she reached up gentle fingers to touch the swelling bruise.

Margaret Smithson looked at her, blindly, uncomprehendingly, as though she did not even hear. "You rang your bell, Miss. What can I get for you?" she said in a steady monotone.

Nell ignored this, trying to coax the poor creature to be seated in the low wicker chair which stood near the window. After a moment or two, the warm sympathy, the soft little pats and the broken exclamations of pity seemed to reach her, and she allowed herself to be installed in the chair, with a soft shawl tucked over her knees, while Nell rummaged frantically in a drawer for a pot of herbal balm of Emma's brewing with which to anoint the bruise. She began to smear it gently over the woman's cheek, chattering all the while of such inconsequential details as the ingredients of the balm and Emma's superstitious notions about picking the various simples at certain phases of the moon, of anything in fact that might distract the poor soul from her tormented thoughts, and wondering the while what else she could offer in the way of help or comfort. One could not go on for ever smoothing ointment into a bruise. She put the jar down on the dressing table, dipped a clean handkerchief into the ewer of cool water that stood on the washstand, and began to bathe the swollen eyes. Miss Smithson simply sat still and suffered her attentions with neither thanks nor protest, but at least the dreadful working of her mouth had stopped.

Rather tentatively Nell next removed the stiff cap, and picking up one of her brushes began to smooth the straggling ends of hair into their accustomed neatness. "You have such pretty hair," she said gently. "It seems a pity that you should always have to hide it under a cap."

The effect of those innocent words was surprising. It was almost as though she had uttered a powerful incantation. The lax figure stiffened beneath her hands. Colour flowed back into the white face, and the drooping shoulders straightened themselves almost proudly. Quite unknowingly Nell had used words that had once been dear and familiar on the lips of her young lover. He, too, had insisted that she take off her cap, and praised her pretty hair. So long ago. And since then she had existed in dumb misery, crushed and submissive, for what was there to hope for? Tom was gone — to the far Antipodes — and she would never see him again.

Life and hope had stirred within her when he had come back so unexpectedly. But she had been terrified of the danger in which he stood; sure, too, that her uncle and Sir Nicholas were trying to involve him in their schemes. It was never from kindness that her uncle had helped him to a job with Sir Charles Trevannion, for he had no kindness in him. Oh! He had taken her in when she had come to him in her shame and destitution, but only because he could use her, and she had worked like a slave up to the very day of her baby's birth. Like enough 'twas the heavy unaccustomed work at that dreadful tavern in Field Lane that had killed it. And since — since they had moved to Wintringham — she had served him loyally and faithfully, and in ten years she had never had so much as a kind word. He even grudged her the few simple clothes that were necessary for decency.

She knew it had been weak and wrong to shut her eyes to certain very dubious activities that were carried on from the Fleece. Not so much the smuggling. Well — everyone was in that to some extent. Even Parson was known to turn a blind eye. And her uncle didn't seem to take much count of it, except that there'd been strangers hidden once or twice in the ruined cottage out beyond Winchelsea. Then there was Sir Nicholas, whose regular visits seemed to be the signal for her uncle to depart on various unobtrusive journeys. She'd felt uneasy at times, though there was nothing to put a finger on. Not until that nice friendly young gentleman had been murdered had she been really worried and frightened. Since then it seemed as though she just couldn't stop turning things over in her mind, and when Sir Nicholas had brought this kind girl to the inn she had determined to do her best to protect her. But at first everything had seemed pleasant and smooth enough, not to mention that Sir Charles looked to be well up to the task of looking after his promised wife.

Then Tom had come back. And her dim grey world had suddenly dissolved into a bewildering kaleidoscope of hope and fear and anxiety. This morning, when Tom didn't come in for his breakfast as usual, she had asked her uncle what he was doing to be so late. He had answered with a burst of bitter vituperation against Tom, and when she had stared at him, not understanding this sudden animosity, he had struck her across the face, calling her a useless idle slut.

She had run out to the stable, but Tom wasn't there. Only that big groom of Sir Charles's, busy over his master's greys. That wouldn't suit Tom, neither, she thought vaguely. He set great store by those greys. But Tom was nowhere to be found. He wasn't in the harness room, and he wasn't in the tiny attic above it, his sleeping quarters, though his gear was scattered about it in some disorder. That was somehow comforting. At least he hadn't gone off and left her. And then sudden terror had seized her. Suppose he had been murdered, like that other poor young man? In vain she had tried to tell herself that no one — she didn't specify who — had any cause to kill Tom.

Back to the kitchen then, in the silly useless hope that he might have come in, and that she would find him eating the breakfast that was spoiling on the hob. The kitchen was empty of course. Miss had rung her bell, and no one to answer but herself, for young Jenny was nowhere about. Dimly she wondered where everyone had got to this morning as automatically she had moved to answer the bell.

Whatever was she doing, sitting in Miss Easton's chair, letting herself be babied like this? Eyes suddenly alive again met Nell's anxious hazel ones in the mirror. She put up a hand to catch the girl's that was plying the brush, took it gently from her unresisting fingers, and laid it back in its place. Carefully she tucked away the loosened strands of hair and pinned on her cap, then folded the shawl and stood up. Her knees had stopped shaking she found, and her voice was quite composed.

"Thank you, Miss," she said quietly. "I'm sorry I acted a bit dazed like. I think knocking my face must have turned me a bit queer. I'll be all right now. Thank you for being so kind. Was it your breakfast that you were wanting when you rang your bell?"

Nell nodded, more discomfited by this sudden composure than by the hysterical state that had preceded it. "Yes, please," she said rather shyly, and hastily qualified the request by adding, "if it's not too much trouble. I slept late — and I have the headache a little." She blushed furiously as she uttered the mild lie, but Miss Smithson only said that in that case she was very sensible to rest, and that she would bring up breakfast as soon as she could, though she was all behind hand this morning with Jenny not coming. Nell assured her that some bread and butter and coffee was all that she required, and that she was sorry to give her the extra trouble of carrying it upstairs.

"It's no trouble," declared the newly invigorated Miss Smithson. "Your uncle breakfasted very early and is gone off somewhere, and Sir Charles is not yet down. I can easily bring up your breakfast." And away she went to do it, just as though nothing unusual had passed between the two of them.

By the time that Nell had washed her hands and face and tidied her sleep rumpled hair, she was back with a tray, on which, Nell was pleased to note, her frugal suggestions had been amplified by a dish of apricot preserve and a bowl of cherries, while the coffee jug was flanked by a tiny pitcher of fresh cream.

She settled herself to the enjoyment of her breakfast, putting the tray on the window ledge, and sitting where she could keep watch on the stable yard. She was presently cheered by the sight of Giles who strolled whistling out of the stable as though he had not a care in the world and established himself on a bench in the sun with a pile of tack to clean. In a little while she saw Miss Smithson go out to him, carrying a tankard and a plate of substantial looking sandwiches. The two of them talked for a few moments and then Miss Smithson returned to the inn. Giles watched her out of sight with a thoughtful expression, but then applied himself zestfully to the tankard. Whatever had passed between them, Giles did not appear to be unduly disturbed, so there could be no cause for Nell to be anxious either.

But when Miss Smithson returned to collect the breakfast tray, it seemed that she was very worried indeed. It appeared that she had sent Jim upstairs with Sir Charles's shaving water and he had received no reply to his knock. Jim having gone off with his master, she had taken up another supply of hot water herself, and when there was no reply to her repeated knocking, had tried the door. Finding it unlocked she had gone in, to the discovery that the room was empty and Sir Charles's bed had not been slept in. Sir Charles's man had assured her that there was no cause for alarm, saying that his master was probably at Trevannions and would undoubtedly turn up safe and sound in his own good time. But she couldn't help being anxious, she confided to Nell, because Tom Ransome appeared to be missing too, and yet all the horses were still in the stables. She looked hopefully at Nell as though expecting her to offer a reasonable explanation of why a man should go off with his groom but without his horses.

Nell was guiltily aware that although she knew the answer she could hardly disclose it to Miss Smithson. She could only shake her head in puzzled fashion and murmur rather feebly that one never knew what men would be at. Miss Smithson then broached the real cause of her anxiety, mentioning the young man who had been murdered, and saying that she feared some similarly dreadful fate might have overtaken the two absentees.

Despite her knowledge of the events of the previous evening and her faith that Giles would not be calmly cleaning tack if his master were in any danger, Nell found that she could not quite repress a foolish tremor at this horrid suggestion, but she did her best to reassure Miss Smithson, and then to give her thoughts a new direction by asking if Jenny had arrived yet. This answered well, Miss Smithson explaining that Jenny, the eldest of a large family, had felt very unwell on the previous day and had probably by now succumbed to the feverish sore throat that had been afflicting her several brothers and sisters for the past week.

"Then I shall come and help you in the kitchen," declared Nell firmly, quite forgetting her supposed headache. "I like kitchens — and I'm sure yours is a nice one. Emma lets me help her sometimes. She says it is always useful to be able to cook."

Miss Smithson was obviously torn between her longing for the comfort of human society and the gross impropriety of permitting Nell to help in the kitchen. "I don't think — " she was beginning, when Nell broke in impetuously.

"Please don't say no. I don't like being alone, and both Sir Charles and Emma have assured me that I would be quite safe with you."

"Well — maybe I could set a chair for you by the kitchen door," suggested Miss Smithson. "It's pretty there, with the hollyhocks and the roses, and you could do your sewing or write letters if you wished. I'll not deny I'd be glad of company this morning."

The two of them spent the rest of the forenoon in rather uneasy companionship. Each felt nothing but good will towards the other, but both had secrets to keep, and every topic of conversation seemed to be set with traps. After Giles had managed, while her companion's back was turned, to bestow upon Nell a reassuring nod, and a conspiratorial jerk of the head in the direction where Trevannions might be supposed to lie, she was able to feel perfectly comfortable about Charles's safety, though she couldn't help wishing he would come back. It was rather a galling admission to one of her independent spirit, but she felt both safer and braver when Charles was at hand, especially when her uncle or Rudd were in the vicinity.

However just at present the inn dozed peacefully in the midday heat, and there was nothing to fear. Indeed Nell, having declined an offer of luncheon because, after her late breakfast and lazy morning, she wasn't hungry, was almost asleep in her chair. Miss Smithson, who seemed incapable of being still, had completed all the preparations for the evening meal and was now making bread, explaining to Nell the various processes involved in producing the delicious crusty loaves that she enjoyed so much, when they heard the sound of a vehicle approaching the inn.

Nell sat up abruptly. Miss Smithson's quiet monologue ceased, though she went on kneading the dough. Nell hoped uneasily that it was not the landlord. He would be bound to wonder what she was doing in the kitchen quarters, and she found his oily geniality both distasteful and somehow frightening. There was not long to wait. The approaching footsteps were not the crisp decisive ones of Sir Charles, nor the heavier tread of the landlord. Round the corner came familiar workaday Jim Cooke. But since he was heading towards them with an air of unusual importance, perhaps he was the bearer of a message. Both ladies awaited his disclosures with deep and anxious interest, but his opening remarks were disappointingly commonplace.

"Muster Rudd won't be 'ome till nightfall, missus. We took a couple barrels over to Tilstowe, and'e've stopped there. Seemingly 'e and Mus' Dunn 'ave business together."

Since Simon Dunn of Tilstowe farm was a leading spirit among the smuggling fraternity, the message was perfectly comprehensible to Miss Smithson, who nodded understanding. But Jim was not finished. Addressing himself to Nell, he went on, "And Mistress Woodstead says will you be sure to stop by at Springbourne today, seeing as you didn't get to see her yesterday, and she's got something special to show you."

His burden delivered he stood regarding the two ladies hopefully, and ignoring Miss Smithson's dismissive nod said eagerly, "I was thinking p'rhaps Miss would let me drive 'er over to Springbourne if so be as the captain ain't 'andy."

Nell guessed that this would be a much pleasanter way of spending an afternoon than the heavy tasks that were Jim's usual portion. She smiled and promised to remember his kind offer, but thought it unlikely that she would require his services. Captain Trevannion would probably be back in good time. Jim trailed away disconsolate. Miss Smithson finished kneading her dough and set it to rise.

The day wore slowly on towards afternoon. Giles and Jim came into the kitchen where despite the heat of the day they disposed of generous helpings of meat pudding and vegetables. Nell left them to enjoy their meal in comfort, feeling that her presence might be an embarrassment, and went up to her room where she fidgetted about restlessly, not knowing quite what she wanted to do. She stood for a while gazing out of the window. The road to Springbourne and to distant Trevannions stretched white and empty. Nothing moved upon it. Presently Giles came out, moved his bench into a patch of shade cast by the stable, sat himself down, propped his shoulders against the wall, and appeared to drift off into peaceful slumber.

If only something would happen. It was this waiting about with nothing to do that fretted her nerves. There had not even been an opportunity for private talk with Giles. If she were to ask him to drive her over to Springbourne to visit Emma he would at least be able to tell her what had happened after Charles had left her last night.

With this in mind she decided to change her muslin dress for one of fine cambric in her favourite shade of green, more suitable for carriage exercise, spinning out the task as long as she could in the hope that any minute would bring Charles cantering along the road. This reminded her that, absorbed as she had been in Miss Smithson's woeful condition, she had not yet thought to enquire about poor Marquis. He must be all right though, or Giles would not be sleeping so peacefully in the shade. She eyed him almost resentfully, and was quite surprised, when she finally made her way downstairs, to find him rising to greet her as though he had not been asleep at all. His hearing must be acute indeed if the sound of her little kid slippers had roused him.

It was disappointing to find that he did not look with favour on her proposed expedition. Master Charles, he explained, strolling with her towards the gate where they would not be overheard, had instructed him to look after her. But his first duty was to keep watch on Sir Nicholas and the landlord, and this he could best do by staying where he was. Though he was diffident about saying it as bluntly as he would have liked, he did not think Nell ought to go visiting, and whatever Emma wanted with her must just wait.

In her heart Nell felt that he was probably right, but she was weary of inaction and did not see that she could possibly come to any harm driving along a couple of miles of quiet country road. She need not even be alone. Jim would be only too glad to go with her.

"Not handling the master's cattle he won't," said Giles, thinking that would be the end of the matter.

"Of course not," returned Nell, very cool and dignified, "the cob will be rested by now. Jim can drive me in the gig. There can be no objection to that."

Giles scratched his head. "I don't like

it, Miss Nell. If I could take you myself 'twould be different. But I reckon I ought to wait here till Master Charles shows his front. Those were my orders, and I don't want to queer his game by going agin them. As for Jim, he's a decent enough lad, but slow in the uptake. There's no knowing how he would show in a crisis," and he shook his head in renewed disapprobation.

Nell was in a strange mood. Anxiety, danger and a half acknowledged love had all taken their toll of her natural resilience. The events of yesterday had wrought her to a high peak of anticipation. Today, she had felt, dreaming in the sunshine, must surely bring a climax — an answer to all her doubts and difficulties. If the truth must be confessed she was not especially worried about her uncle, having complete faith in Charles's ability to protect her from his machinations. But her burgeoning love for Charles was a very different matter. Shyly she had thought that perhaps he would come to her today — that the kiss he had pressed on her hand was the prelude to a formal declaration. He would suggest that their mock betrothal should become a true one, and then — and then — At this point her dreams offered so many ecstatic possibilities that she blushed at her own imaginings, and reminded herself severely that Charles could not come to her until his duty was accomplished, and that she must be patient.

So she had waited. And nothing had happened. As the hours passed without news, the bright confidence of the morning faded, and the brooding atmosphere of the inn seemed to grow more menacing. Now she was at the limit of her endurance. Charles seemed to have vanished into the blue. Giles was being awkward and would not help her. All she wanted was to escape from this horrible inn and find Emma. In that safe haven she could sob out her loneliness and her fears and frustration and be comforted.

She eyed Giles frostily and announced her fixed intention of having Jim drive her over to Springbourne at once.

"Now there's no need to get on your high ropes, Miss Nell," retorted that insubordinate creature with infuriating indulgence. "If you're so set on going, I can't stop you. We'll just have to hope no harm comes of it. I'll tell Jim to harness the cob."

Seated in the gig, with the air cooling her hot cheeks and the delighted Jim handling the reins, Nell began to feel better. It was refreshing just to have escaped from the restraint of the Fleece and even from the supervision of Giles. For a little while she simply relaxed, enjoying the sensation of movement and freedom, and studying Jim's driving methods with considerable interest. He could scarcely be described as a top sawyer she acknowledged with a twitch of amusement. Neck or nothing was more his style. And it was at this point in her observations that it was suddenly borne in upon her that he was shaking with barely suppressed laughter. For a moment she couldn't help wondering if he had been sampling the Fleece's home brew rather too freely during his master's absence, but he handled the stolid cob competently enough, and it was not until they reached the Springbourne fork that she had any real cause to suppose that his judgement was impaired. When, however, he turned the gig without hesitation down the Winchelsea road, it seemed to be time to make a stand.

"Jim — stop!" she said urgently. "This isn't the way to the Lamb. For goodness sake give me the reins. You must be completely foxed!"

This very improper term on the lips of a lady provoked the explosion of unbridled merriment that had been threatening ever since they left the Fleece. Jim threw back his head and roared, until finally he doubled up in wheezing gasps, the tractable animal between the shafts obligingly easing to a gentle amble as soon as he felt the reins loose on his back.

Nell drew a deep indignant breath and prepared to give the drunken reprobate the full benefit of her opinion. She was forestalled.

"Oh Miss! Didn't I bubble them both just fine?" he begged ecstatically. "I did it just right — just the way he told me, and they never suspicioned a thing. 'Don't be pushful,' he says. 'Just offer to drive her over to Springbourne. If she won't, she won't, but it's worth a try.' And I done it just right, just the way he said."

Nell stared at him, only half listening, and, since he spoke in broadest dialect, comprehending less. "Look, Jim," she repeated patiently, "will you please turn about? I want to go to Springbourne, to the Lamb, to see Mistress Woodstead."

Jim gathered up the reins willingly enough. "Aye, Miss. But it's not to Mistress Emma that I'm taking you. We're going to meet Sir Charles."

16

LIFE in the country, under his present circumstances, was really very wearing, decided Sir Nicholas. Even the simplest tasks seemed to require his personal supervision — just the one thing he had hoped to avoid. He really disliked physical violence very much, indeed, and to be forced into contact with it would be most unpleasant, but he could no longer foresee any possibility of avoiding such contact. He was also extremely tired. The previous day had been singularly frustrating. Having wasted hours of valuable time in establishing an alibi which was to prove totally unnecessary, he had then been forced to pass an insipid evening in the society of his niece. Even the solace of slumber had been denied him, by the need to establish the whereabouts of Trevannion and Tom Ransome, and in this exercise he had been unsuccessful. The pair of them had simply vanished without trace.

Finally he had had to endure the scorn of that bacon-brain, Rudd, who, just because he had not been a party to this particular attempt, had roundly declared that any man of ordinary common sense would have known that such a chancy business was foredoomed to failure. Sir Nicholas decided that he was getting rather tired of Mr. Rudd.

He had been able to snatch barely three hours sleep, and that had been much troubled by dreams. Possibly the buttered crab had been injudicious, but a man of his epicurean tastes grew a little weary of Miss Smithson's plain fare, and dinner at the George had served the secondary purpose of demonstrating his presence some miles from Wintringham.

He had risen early, and having ascertained from Rudd that there was still no sign of the absentees had realised that he might shortly need to abandon his snug quarters at the Fleece. If Ransome had made his attempt and failed, it would not take Sir Charles long to choke the truth out of him. Fortunately he knew nothing of real importance, but he could scarcely fail to direct suspicion at Sir Nicholas. It would be wise to ensure that no evidence was available to prove that his visits to the Fleece were anything but innocent. Thoughtfully he rehearsed an air of mild surprise. "Why sir — the locality happens to suit my constitution. And when one is compelled to ruralise — " A slight shrug there, and perhaps a hint of a man-of-the-world smile. It would all depend on the quality of his interrogator. But it would not come to that.

Carefully he sorted through his papers, setting aside one or two that would be better destroyed. Harmless enough in themselves, they yet pointed the fact that he had easy access to more vital information. There was a mass of personal papers, accounts and such, that were of no interest to anyone but himself. These he replaced in the small coffer that held his writing materials. A man with no papers at all would be highly suspect. Finally he came to the slim packet which the Bonapartist agent had rejected. This gave him seriously to think. The information it contained had been obtained at some risk and considerable cost. And if the fortunes of war swung against the Allies, as they had so often done before, it might yet fetch its price. He could not bring himself to destroy it. But it must certainly be bestowed in a safer place. The ruined cottage on the inlet where the French agents had lain concealed might serve. None of the local folk went near it since it was reputedly haunted, and in any case was so tumbledown that it was actually dangerous if one did not know it well. There would be some niche or crevice where he could hide his incriminating treasure.

Meanwhile he bestowed it safely in an inner pocket and went down to the coffee room for a leisurely breakfast. His niece did not put in an appearance. Possibly she still had the headache. But the time was not yet ripe for the administration of his 'cachets'. He must first have a clearer view of the general situation. The present uncertainty he found irritating, for though he detected in himself a natural genius for improvisation, yet he was by preference a man of orderly habits, who liked to have his course well planned in advance. Well — the day must certainly bring news of Sir Charles, and then he could decide what was best to be done. Meanwhile he would ride gently towards the coast and dispose of his precious package. The coffee room fire had already accepted the other débris of his morning's work.

The cottage proved to be regrettably ill furnished with hiding places, though in other respects well suited to his purpose. Built a hundred years earlier for a retired sea captain — a gentleman who had first risen to fame and fortune as one of Morgan's buccaneers, but who, like his master, had later turned respectable — it had originally consisted of a ground floor of three rooms opening out of each other. From the middle one of the three a steep staircase led to a loft above which ran the length of the building. The original owner had spent much of his time here, for the seaward wall was pierced by several narrow unglazed windows, which permitted him to smell the sea and keep an eye on the channel shipping. From the central room, on the ground floor, a trap door gave access to a cellar below.

After the old man's death the place had passed through various hands. At some time the apertures in the loft had been roughly blocked up because they were thought to make the place damp. It had stood empty now for years and during this time one end wall had collapsed after an exceptionally high spring tide. The derelict kitchen, perched on the edge of the chasm, yawned widely at the passer-by across a waste of soil and rubble. The roof had been roughly shored up with stout timbers, but the side door had gone with the falling wall, and the only other entrance, set in the centre of the landward frontage, had been boarded over.

It was, however, perfectly possible to obtain access to the interior of the building by a route known only to initiates, a dark and malodorous gallery leading from a concealed entrance on the shore to the cellar beneath the cottage. But since this entrance was submerged at half tide it was necessary to select one's visiting times with care and not to prolong one's visit unduly, since delay might mean incarceration in the mouldering dwelling till next low water. Sir Nicholas, having negotiated the intricacies of the passage with due care, strolled from room to room seeking a safe hold for his precious package. It was more difficult than he had anticipated. The wrecked kitchen offered a number of promising fissures in crumbling stonework, but though difficult and dangerous it was not impossible for some adventurous urchin to scramble across the débris of the landslip. The other two rooms, stripped of their furnishing save such as was worn beyond repair, presented only a desolation of damp stained walls and yawning hearths. He did investigate the latter, but it proved impossible to reach high enough inside them to ensure the safety of the documents.

As a last resort he climbed the steep stairway that led to the loft, cursing his own lack of forethought in neglecting to bring up a lantern from the cellar, for the place was in almost total darkness. Just here and there splinters of light penetrated between the rough wood and stone that had been used to block the loopholes, and by this feeble illumination he picked his way to the far end of the room where one aperture, as he had good reason to know, was only shuttered. Fumbling in the darkness and swearing at a torn fingernail, he succeeded at last in lifting down the rough boards and admitting a shaft of daylight. And now at last his efforts were rewarded. Lintels and jambs had been roughly cut from blocks of sandstone, and the neglect of years had caused cracks to appear where the masoned stone met the rubble filled wall. Many of these were only superficial, but eventually he found one ideally suited to his purpose. By folding the documents into a narrow compass he was able to thrust them well out of sight into the thickness of the wall. Should he ever wish to retrieve them a few minutes brisk work with a crowbar would be all that was needed.

He dusted his fingers fastidiously and lingered a moment or two gazing out at the peaceful sunlit scene framed by the opening in the stone. The house had been carefully sited. Though it faced seaward, yet the range of vision from his loophole covered both arms of the little bay and commanded the approach roads on both sides. At the moment all was still. No living thing moved in the sun-tranced landscape and only the calls of the gulls and the moan of a distant ewe broke the utter silence. Sir Nicholas paid passing tribute to the sound military instinct of the man who had ordered the building. For a moment he wondered idly what the fellow's past had been that he should have taken such pains to secure himself against approach by stealth. Then he shrugged. The man had been dust a hundred years. Suffice it that his stronghold had served a purpose never intended. This loft had proved an excellent refuge and signalling point for the men who had come ashore at slack tide from that shy French fishing vessel.

He took out a pocket knife and carefully trimmed the torn nail, then addressed himself to the task of replacing the boards across the opening. As he did so a distant figure came into sight, topping the crest of the hill that sloped gently to the shore. He paused in his activities, the board resting against the wall, and narrowed his eyes against the dazzle of light. There was something very familiar about the stocky figure padding determinedly down the rough path, and he very soon identified the landlord of the Fleece. A slight frown creased his brow. He would have preferred not to have been discovered in his present situation, but it could not be avoided. The man was bound to recognise his horse which he had left tethered in the shade of a tree, and there was not time for him to pass through the gallery and make good his departure before Rudd caught up with him. In any case it seemed probable that some important development had sent the man in search of him. He finished his task without undue haste, and returned to the former living-room to await events. It was not long before he heard the hollow sound of approaching footsteps and the landlord's head and shoulders appeared through the trap opening.

"Aye! Hoped I'd find you here," the man puffed, as he climbed the last two or three steps and dropped the trap back into position with a thud. "'Twas just chance young Jim said he'd seen you ride out this a-way. I was main glad to see your nag and know you was still here." His eyes roved the room and Sir Nicholas's person with curiosity, wondering what had brought him to this queer place by daylight.

However there was no time to dwell on this mystery. Sir Nicholas was waiting impatiently, and he himself was big with news.

"I've found 'em," he announced importantly. "Leastways I reckon I know where they're to *be* found. There's no doubting the luck's on our side in this round, else why should I choose this very morning to take a couple o' kegs o' cider over to Simon Dunn? I been meaning to do it these days past seeing as he'll be wanting it for the harvest time, but if I 'adn't just 'appened to pick on this morning, 'e might never 'ave thought to tell me about the strange chap that came knocking on 'is door last night. Late on it was, and they all abed, but Simon do be used to later callers, so down 'e comes. And there's this chap, a great giant of a fellow, wanting to 'ire 'is cart and the old mare along of it for the night. A queer set-out Simon thought. But this cove being very free with 'is blunt — told Simon to name 'is own price 'e did — the bargain was struck. Only Simon, being curious like, slips out of the dairy entry and follows to see where the chap makes for. And blow me if 'e don't 'ead for the Fleece! Don't drive right up though, like any honest customer. 'E stops in the lane. And then another tall cove pops up from under the 'edge, and between 'em they 'oists a third chap into the cart, and away they goes towards the Rye road — and to Trevannions I make no doubt, though in course I didn't tell Simon so. Simon goes back 'ome to 'is bed, but first thing in the morning 'e goes to look, and there's mare and cart, just as the fellow 'ad promised. And cart floor's been scrubbed. Seems like there might 'ave been blood stains, and someone mighty anxious they shouldn't be seen."

"The 'great giant of a fellow' being Trevannion's groom," murmured Sir Nicholas, "and he and Trevannion shifting Ransome's body. He was dead, I suppose?"

The landlord shook his head. "Not

then, so far as Simon could make out. He was tied up, and some kind of a muffler over his face. Well you don't tie up a corpse, do you? Stands to reason."

"So doubtless by now he has told all he knows. Well — there's little danger. They can prove nothing, and no one will listen to the ravings of an escaped convict."

"That's as maybe. But Captain Trevannion knows who's behind the attempt on him. I reckon we got to deal with that lad, and smartish, too. So I've taken steps, as you might say."

Sir Nicholas stiffened. If this clumsy oaf had meddled in what was a very delicate business, there might indeed be real danger. "And pray what steps did you deem necessary?" he asked softly.

"Well first of all I've fixed it with young Jim to bring the lass here, that's if he can get 'er off without a fuss, and I reckon 'e'll manage that. That there groom is sniffing round the Fleece like a terrier at a rat run. There'll be no shifting 'im till either you or me shows up again. And when Jim tells the wench that Sir Charles wants 'er to meet 'im, she'll jump at it like a cock at a gooseberry.

Once she's safe in our 'ands, 'e's bound to come after 'er. And there couldn't be a better place than this for dealing with the pair of them."

Sir Nicholas listened to this simple exposition with mingled fury and contempt. "And if Sir Charles has already returned to the Fleece, as seems more than probable, what happens then to your precious Jim and his story?"

"Ah, but 'e won't 'ave done," replied the landlord confidently. "I put it to Simon Dunn that 'e was on the track of the Gentlemen, nosing out the places where we store the stuff till we can get it away. Proper put about, Simon was. He's posting two or three of the lads on the road 'twixt Rye and Wintringham, and if my fine gentleman comes back before we're ready for 'im, 'e'll like as not get the horse shot from under 'im. And if the bullet goes astray and does for 'im — well so much the better says I. They can't stay on the job much after mid-afternoon though. They're shifting the stuff that was stored by Cock Marling tonight, and the lads are going to lay a false trail out towards Pett. They'll need to get ready for that."

Sir Nicholas considered the plan carefully. It trusted far too much to the element of chance. Jim might not succeed, for quite a variety of reasons, in luring the girl into the trap, and everything hinged on that. Sir Charles might return to the inn by a different route, and so escape the ambush laid for him. Since, however, his own participation was not required in these hazardous early stages, he was prepared to watch the development of the plan with benevolent interest. If the luck was indeed on their side, he would turn Rudd's intervention to good account. But there was no doubt that the fellow was getting above himself. Something would have to be done about him.

"And if all goes as you hope, how do you propose to deal with your prisoners?" be asked.

"Knock 'em on the head and set fire to the place," replied the landlord, with the pleased air of the man who has thought of everything. "The traders have used it long enough — it's risky to keep on using the same place — and too many people know about the cellar entrance."

Sir Nicholas nodded. The plan was crude, but effective enough, given a modicum of luck. People might wonder why two, or possibly three charred bodies should be discovered in a presumably empty house, but there was no need for him to fatigue his brain with the invention of a plausible tale. Local rumour would soon do that, and in superfluity. He need only lend his support to the tale he considered most credible. Carefully he searched the plan for obvious flaws. He thought regretfully of his hidden treasure. It would almost certainly be reduced to ashes in the projected holocaust, but its loss would be trivial in comparison with the fortune he would gain by successfully disposing of his niece.

"What about the lad, Jim? He's going to know too much for safety."

"Not for long 'e ain't," said Rudd laconically. "Once 'e's brought Missy safely to her trysting place, 'e's of no further use. I'd 'ave liked to use 'im to make sure the captain got the office, but it's too risky. We'll 'ave to rely on them spotting the gig. I'll make sure it's left in plain sight. No. The lad must bum with the rest. We can drop the other two easy enough. They can only come through the trap one at a time. And if so be as Jim sends the lass up the passage on 'er own, I'll tend to 'im myself when t'other business is done with. Never you fear, Sir Nicholas, 'e'll be put to bed with a shovel all right, and nobody to raise riot and rumpus about 'im neither, seeing as 'ow 'e's only a foundling brat," and in excess of joviality over his own cleverness he actually had the brazen assurance to slap Sir Nicholas on the shoulder.

Not by the flicker of an eyelash did Sir Nicholas betray the seething fury that filled him at this presumptuous familiarity. With seeming carelessness he strolled over to the window, shrugging off that importunate hand. "Damp as it is," he said thoughtfully, "the place won't burn easily. Can you readily lay your hands on any combustibles that would help the fire get a hold?"

Apparently this need had escaped Rudd's calculations, for he spent a few moments in thinking it over before pronouncing that the few remnants of wooden furniture, with the old straw mattress out of the sleeping chamber and driftwood that could be brought up from the shore would form a useful nucleus for the bonfire, and a couple of barrels of oil, suitably disposed, would ensure that it gained a hold on doors and roof timbers. He engaged himself to provide the necessary fuel in good time, and presently went off to see about it, leaving Sir Nicholas to his own reflections.

17

SO he had not forgotten her, nor despised her assistance. Nell hugged the joyful thought to herself as the gig rattled and lurched its way along the rough track. She had no idea where they were going, except that they were travelling south-west and following the line of the coast. No faintest doubt of Jim's good faith clouded her eager anticipation of the moment when she would meet Charles once more. Jim, face wreathed in an ecstatic grin at the memory of the ease with which he had carried out his instructions, devoted all his attention to the uneven terrain. Conversation would have been difficult in any case, and Nell had no particular desire for it, being wholly absorbed in her own delightful thoughts. Perhaps Jim did ponder the oddity of commencing an elopement from a derelict house that was notoriously difficult of access. His master's strangely uncharacteristic behaviour in helping the young lovers to their odd trysting place was easily explained. Sir Charles must have been uncommon generous about greasing him in the fist. He wondered what Sir Nicholas would say when he discovered that the love birds had eluded him and were well on the way to the border. Jim had no great liking for Sir Nicholas. A nasty cutting way he had of speaking to a fellow as though he was dirt, and never so much as a shilling slipped into a lad's hand. Jim would be quite pleased to see Sir Nicholas out-jockeyed.

Nell's thoughts were entirely centred on Charles. Since she had no idea that Jim had received his orders from the landlord, or that he believed himself to be assisting at an elopement, her mind was full of the wildest conjecture as to what necessity had caused Charles to summon her to his aid. She wished she had worn riding dress — he might need to send her on some urgent errand — and that she had brought her pistol, since that too might be needed before the adventure was done. But over and above these excited imaginings was the thought of being once more at Charles's side, helping him, obeying his orders, perhaps receiving a precious word of commendation. Surely, surely, he must truly value her, since he had sent for to help him? Lost in a romantic dream, in which, by means unspecified, *she* was the one who brought all his plans to a successful issue, and far more concerned with the warm and loving look in his eyes than with the importance of those plans, Nell suffered the jolting of the gig over the slippery turf without even noticing.

Presently they stopped beside a gate. "We 'as to walk from 'ere," Jim explained, as he hitched the reins to the gatepost. Nell jumped down without assistance and stared wonderingly around. Apart from a tumbledown building which she took to be a barn, there was no visible habitation. Where was Charles? She would have liked to question her guide about his dealings with her beloved, but since she did not know how far he had been admitted into Charles's confidence, it seemed wiser to preserve a discreet silence. So she followed him without demur through the gate and down a path that was little more than a sheep track.

"'Tis tedious rough walking for a lady," he said, holding aside a trailing plant that obstructed the path, "and I doubt the wet sand'll spoil your slippers, but it's the only way of getting into the place since the land slip," and he jerked his head towards the building that now loomed above them.

"Are we to go in there?" demanded Nell, surprised. "Why — I'm sure I saw a door at the back. Could we not have used that?"

Jim shook his head wisely. "It's all nailed up, Miss," he explained. "We 'as to go in through the cellars. But it's not dark," he offered cheerfully. "There's plenty candles to light the way. I guess it's been used by the Gentlemen, days past, though 'tain't now of course."

Here was romance and adventure indeed. A secret assignation in a smuggler's hold. Eyes wide and bright with excitement, Nell stared around the narrow entrance, noticing several footprints in the fine sand that the receding tide had left on its floor. Jim explained that it was low tide just now, so the entrance would be usable for some four or five hours. "So you'll need to be away before then," he finished with a knowing grin, and showed her where the roughly cut gallery steps led upwards.

As he had promised, it was sufficiently lit. There were candles stuck on spikes which had been hammered into the rock. But it was far from inviting, the lower steps being wet and slimy with weed, the walls glistening with ooze, and the whole aspect dank and dismal, while the candles flickered in the constant draught and filled the narrow passage with oily smoke and the reek of tallow. For all her courage, Nell was glad to accept Jim's obliging offer to lead the way, and for the first time a touch of doubt clouded her eager spirits. What could have caused Charles to bring her to such a place?

This was no time for missish qualms and tremors she told herself, with an impatient shake of the head, and summoned her energies to following Jim's reassuringly sturdy legs as they led the way upward. Once or twice he turned and gave her a helping hand over the steeper rises, and so brought her safely to the cellar below the house. Here a lanthorn hung on a wall peg, and Nell's spirits began to rise again as she perceived signs of human occupation. Several barrels stood in one corner of the room, and a pile of driftwood roughly stacked, as well as just such items of outworn or broken furniture as one would expect to find relegated to the attics or cellars of the house. But there was no time to study her surroundings in detail. Jim was already climbing the steep stone stair that led to the room above, and she watched him struggling to raise the heavy trap door. He managed it eventually, but there was no ensuing gleam of brighter light. The room above must be in darkness. She watched Jim climb the remaining steps, lifting the trap clear and holding it in front of him as he disappeared out of her sight. There was a thud. That would be Jim dropping the trap cover. She thought she heard him speak to someone, and then suddenly bright daylight shone down through the opening. Jim must have drawn back the curtains and let in the light so that she could see her way more clearly. Eagerly, gaily, she ran up the stair and stepped into the room. In one brief shocked glance she saw its desolation. Not the curtains of her imagining but an old straw mattress, tattered and soiled, its filling exuding from a dozen rents, had been used to darken the window. It now leaned drunkenly against the wall. Stretched on the floor in the light from the window lay the body of Jim Cooke, face down in the dust. She took one swift impulsive step towards him, then stopped and turned, slowly, reluctantly, cold terror at her heart, knowing already what she must inevitably see. Leaning gracefully against the chimney piece, casual and impassive as ever, Sir Nicholas met her frightened bewildered stare without visible emotion. Beside him was Bart Rudd, all agrin at the success of his plot.

"So the little lovebird flew straight into the trap," jeered Rudd, and came towards her. Nell sprang for the opening in a desperate bid for escape, but it was just this expected reaction that he had moved to block. His great hands caught her up without effort and carried her, fighting wildly, to the hearth, where he stood her on her feet, face to face with her uncle, and twisted her hands roughly behind her back, where he controlled them easily in one of his huge paws while he flung the other arm round her writhing twisting body. She kicked out furiously, stamping on his feet and hacking at his shins, but her little feet in their soft kid slippers could do no effective damage. He merely pulled her closer against his body and used both arms to subdue her struggles, trapping her hands against him and saying in oily admiration, "My! What a fierce little lovebird it is. Lie still now, my pretty. Your uncle don't like to see you so put about. Old Bart won't hurt you."

Nell's struggles ceased. It was useless and foolish to wear herself out against his enormous strength, when she might later need all her energies for an attempt at escape. Her first wild flurry of resistance had been inspired more by her instinctive revulsion from the brute who was holding her than from any real hope of escaping him. She stood still. Rudd, deciding that she had acknowledged defeat, relaxed his grip a little, and took the opportunity to pass an appreciative hand over the curve of her breast.

The furtive movement did not escape Sir Nicholas, and it annoyed him. He had listened with equanimity, even with mild amusement, to Rudd's suggestion that they should sell the girl to a brothel. This was different. She was a damned nuisance, and he must of necessity encompass her death. But she was of his blood, and he would not see her mishandled by this coarse oaf.

"Let her go," he said, quietly enough, but there was a note in his voice that caused Rudd's hands to drop away from the girl's body as though they had been stung. "She cannot escape now, and there is no reason why she should be man-handled and insulted." And turning to the girl, he went on in the same cold gentle voice, "If you had only permitted yourself to be guided by me, there would have been no need to proceed to these unpleasant lengths. You would have been safely in the care of your good aunt. As it is, I fear you have several extremely uncomfortable hours ahead of you. We must hope that the experience will bring you to a more biddable frame of mind. You will be good enough to climb the stairway behind you there, which leads to the room above this. There you will remain, until I have decided how I shall bestow you."

Nell looked at the stairway, and hesitated. The thought of rendering meek obedience made her hot with shame, but what choice had she? Even as she meditated a frantic appeal, Sir Nicholas said gently, "If you do not obey me, our worthy Rudd here shall carry you to your room. But I am sure you would be loath to put him to so much trouble."

The words of appeal died on her lips. She directed a glance of burning disgust at the pair of them, and walked steadily to the stairs. Only when she had climbed them and opened the door to perceive the dark cavern of her prison did she turn her head towards her uncle and say, with a cool composure that matched his own, "Am I to be permitted a light in my imprisonment?"

Sir Nicholas shrugged indifferently, but as she stood quietly waiting, he at last reached down a lanthorn from its peg on the wall and kindled a light which he set to the stump of candle inside it. This he handed to the silent girl. She uttered no word of thanks, simply took it from his extended hand and closed the door behind her. Sir Nicholas lifted into position the heavy bar which passed across the entire door frame, fitting into supports at either side, and making it quite impossible to open the door from within. The bait was held securely in the trap. Now to see if the rest of the scheme would work.

He came leisurely down the stairs, and, ignoring the landlord, crossed over to the sprawled body of the unfortunate dupe, whom he stirred, not ungently, with one foot. Rudd came across to join him, and seizing the lad's shoulders, rolled him on to his back. Blood from an ugly wound at the side of his head had trickled across his face and mingled with the dust to form a grotesque, horribly patched mask. His eyes were closed, but he was still breathing. Rudd's hand went out to the club which he had dropped after using it so effectively. "Didn't hit him hard enough," he grunted, and it was obvious that he proposed to correct that error forthwith. Sir Nicholas, who did not share his actual pleasure in violence and cruelty, and had no wish to see coldblooded murder committed before his eyes, put out a detaining hand.

"No need for that — as yet," he said. "Later, perhaps." And then, as though proffering some excuse for his squeamishness, added thoughtfully, "It won't do for him to be found battered to death if he's supposed to have perished in a fire. Even the blow you have already inflicted will have to be accounted for."

"Eh! 'Tis simple enough. The poor lad fell down the stairs in his haste to escape from the flames," suggested Rudd piously. "Maybe if I was to drop him down now," nodding at the still open trap, "it would finish the job nicely without upsetting your honour."

"Yes. And leave his body lying there to warn Trevannion I suppose," retorted Sir Nicholas, slightly ruffled by the sneering reference to his delicate sensibilities. "Do you imagine he would just calmly step over the corpse and come on up the stairs without giving it a second thought?"

Rudd muttered some obscenity under his breath, but made no further objection when Sir Nicholas bade him tie the fellow up without more ado, though he tightened the knots with cruel force, and for good measure muffled the lad's unconscious face with his own bloodstained neckerchief, expressing a wish that he might suffocate. He then dragged the body into the adjoining room which had served as the long dead captain's sleeping cabin and dumped it on the floor. This accomplished he returned to Sir Nicholas, slightly breathless from his exertions, and remarked, with a return to his habitual obsequious manner, "Happen your Honour was in the right of it at that. He's more of a heavyweight than he looks. If I'd once dropped him down that trap, I'd never have got him up again."

Sir Nicholas vouchsafed no reply other than a slight nod. He remained lost in thought for several moments, and then suggested that it might be as well if Rudd went off to buy food for the two of them. "We can scarcely expect any further developments for a couple of hours. By that time the tide will have turned, and I've no wish to be stranded here overnight without suitable provision. A blanket wouldn't come amiss either. It can be devilish chill here after dark."

Rudd objected that he would be obliged to purchase the necessary articles, and that he had not brought his purse, whereupon Sir Nicholas rather grudgingly handed over a couple of guineas. This being satisfactorily settled, Rudd went off on this domestic errand. Sir Nicholas, after contemplating his surroundings with growing dislike, went down to the cellar and succeeded, with considerable exertion, in hauling a small barrel up to the living:room. Upon this he established himself to keep watch through the window, rising from time to time and prowling the length of the room to peer through each window in turn. Nothing stirred. Indoors there was no sound from either of the captives. Without, the hillside drowsed in the late afternoon sunshine. Sir Nicholas resumed his uncomfortable perch, and fixed his thoughts on the bright prospect ahead, when he should have inherited his niece's fortune.

18

IT was past five o'clock when Sir
Charles, on the newly shod Marshall
trotted briskly into the stable yard to
find the place deserted except for Giles,
apparently sound asleep on a bench. At the
sound of hoofs he opened his eyes, got up
in leisurely fashion, and came to take the
horse. But it was no sleep bleared face
that looked anxiously up at Charles.

"Did you see aught of Miss Nell on
the road?" he demanded at once.

Charles swung easily down from the
saddle, to any watching eye a man
conversing idly with his groom, but there
was an overtone of anxiety in his voice
as he said, "No. When did she go out,
and with whom?"

"Soon after two. Young Cooke was
driving her over to Springbourne in the
gig. Seems he brought her a message
from Emma, and she was fair set on
going. But I'd have thought they should
be back by now."

Charles nodded. "I'll give her a few more minutes. She may have stayed overlong with Mistress Woodstead. Women are the devil. I told her to lie close and not to venture out alone."

Giles's grin momentarily banished the anxious frown. "Yes, Sir. So she said. Also that she had done just as you bade her and waited in all morning, but enough was enough."

Charles returned the grin. "Out of frame, was she? Dull work — just waiting. I meant to be back sooner, but I was delayed. How's Marquis?"

They entered the stable together, leaving Marshall hitched to the ring outside, and moved to the far end, Charles's keen glance verifying that no hidden listener lurked in the shadows. A brief inspection showed that Marquis was perfectly recovered, his eye bright, his skin cool and supple to the touch, his black head lifted proudly as he blew loving greetings in his master's face. Charles nodded, well satisfied, and pushed the questing black muzzle gently aside.

"All right, old fellow. Your turn tomorrow. I'll take Marshall," he added to Giles. "We came along quite easily — plenty in him still. I had thought to be back by noon, but I had a visitor, a messenger from our friend Gressingham. Ostensibly to look over my grandfather's stud, and certainly knows one end of a horse from the other. What he really wanted of course was a report on progress, and unfortunately there was very little I could tell him. He seemed to feel that Ransome's attempt to murder me was a most encouraging sign, but was disappointed to learn that he was only a tool and knows nothing of value. I got all I could out of him last night after you'd gone. He was hired to murder me on the pretext that I was a threat to the smuggling fraternity, but out of some mistaken notion of loyalty to his employer he refuses to incriminate Sir Nicholas. My visitor — by the way he claims cousins with me somewhere far back on our family tree — thoroughly approves of Sir Nicholas as chief suspect. It appears that from time to time one or two thoughtful gentlemen have already wondered how he contrived to support the state that he considers appropriate to his rank. His own fortune is known to be modest — indeed scarcely more than a competence — and his wife's portion was not large. But of course none of this is proof. I left my new cousin trying to wring a few more crumbs of information out of Ransome. I doubt he'll not succeed, but he seems well content to ruralise for a day or two, and begged my permission to try out some of the young stock. He's taken a great fancy to Marmion, and would like to buy him. Now" — with an abrupt change of tone and subject — "what do you think that dratted girl is up to? I shan't be easy in my mind till she's safe home. I'll just take Marshall gently along the Springbourne road and make sure all's well. You hold the fort here. No sign of activity?"

"None, Sir. Sir Nicholas went off early this morning, riding the bay. He took the Winchelsea road and is not yet returned. Rudd went off to one of the farms — Tilstowe — which may have been unfortunate, if Dunn talked. He sent back a message that he wouldn't be home till nightfall. I reckon," went on Giles shrewdly, "there's a run on tonight.

Moonset's about midnight. They'll be getting ready for it. But Master Rudd'll be safe back indoors afore the lugger puts in. *He* don't have no truck with smuggling."

"There might be more to it than just plain smuggling," said Charles thoughtfully. "If Sir Nicholas comes back, don't let him out of your sight. Follow him if he goes out again. I'll be back myself as soon as I can, but I must make sure that plaguey brat of mine is safe."

With the words he was in the saddle and trotting out of the gate. Giles stared after him, his eyes crinkled in amusement. So that was how the land lay. The speech had scarcely been loverlike, but Giles knew his master. Well — he had already guessed what was in the wind. The girl was all right, and came of good stock, even if her uncle was a queer nabs. She'd make a good bride for a soldier. It was to be hoped they could hush up the scandal that was like to break over her when her uncle's dealings were revealed. If the worst came to the worst the Captain must just marry her out of hand and carry her out of the country till the talk died down.

Having thus settled his master's future to his own entire satisfaction, Giles stretched his powerful body luxuriously and turned to his own affairs. It looked like being a busy night. A good wash and a shave and a hearty meal would set him up nicely for his labours.

It was fortunate that he put his programme into action immediately, and that Miss Smithson, with no other claim upon her services, was able to set upon the table without delay the sizzling rashers of home cured ham, flanked by fried eggs and fortified by a loaf of newly-baked bread, that were his fancy. For he had scarcely savoured the last delicious mouthful, and was still wondering whether or no it would be judicious to top off his repast with a crust of bread thickly spread with Miss Smithson's celebrated apricot preserve, when his gastronomic dilemma was promptly settled by the thunderous clatter of approaching hoofs. He sprang to the kitchen window to see Marshall coming down the road at full gallop, his rider barely steadying him before they leapt the yard gate and slid to a halt by the stable door. With a speed and neatness surprising in so large a man, he was out of the kitchen and catching Marshall's bridle as Charles flung himself out of the saddle, grim-faced and shaking with fury.

"Emma's not set eyes on her," he said curtly. "She never sent any message, and hasn't spoken with Jim Cooke this sennight."

"And Sir Nicholas and Rudd both gone from here all day," rejoined Giles quietly. "Abduction?"

"Yes. I don't think — They wouldn't dare," he said, determined to banish by reasoned argument the fear of an ultimate horror that could only sap his courage and good sense. "They must know I'd be hot on their trail, and unlike poor Ransome, my credit is pretty good, and my evidence against them would be believed. I think her life *must* be safe until they can dispose of me, though God alone knows in what case we shall find her." This was a thought that did not bear prolonged contemplation. He must concentrate instead on possible action.

"Now, where will they have taken her?" he said, keeping his voice cool by determined effort. "If she left here in the gig she can't be far away, unless they transferred her to a hired chaise, for Sir Nicholas's own carriage is still in the coach house. They'd not have an easy job either, once she realised she'd been tricked. I suppose it's too much to hope that she had her pistol with her?"

Giles shook his head. "I don't know, Sir, but I don't think so. She wasn't wearing a cloak, and I don't see how she could have been carrying a pistol on her without me noticing. She had a sort of little bag on her arm, but not big enough to hold a pistol."

There was a tiny pause, each man pursuing his own uncomfortable thoughts, Giles guilt-stricken because he had allowed Nell to stray from his guardianship, Charles picturing the defiant courage with which she would face her captors, and the brutality with which it would be crushed. Then Giles said, "What about this house Rye way that Sir Nicholas spoke of? Belonged to his wife's aunt didn't it? Would he have taken her there?"

Charles shook his head. "I doubt if it even exists. And I'm pretty sure he would never have mentioned it if he intended to use it. Emma said to ask Miss Smithson to help us — to tell her what has happened. It seems she has already been trying both to protect and to warn Nell, as far as she dared, poor soul." And he moved with long impatient strides towards the kitchen where Miss Smithson was engaged in clearing the débris of Giles's meal. She too had heard the desperate flurry of arrival and looked up from her task as they came in, her face white and strained with anxiety as she sought to read their news on their faces.

"Miss Easton has been abducted," said Charles without preamble, "and we believe her uncle to be behind the affair. Emma Woodstead bade me ask your help, and vowed I could trust you as I would her. Have you any notion where he might have taken her?"

At first it seemed as though she did not understand. She sank down on to a stool and pressed her hands against her face as though to still some intolerable ache, and her hoarsely muttered words seemed to have no connection with his question.

"Oh dear God! That poor young man! Not again. Oh no! Not again."

Charles's eyes widened at this unexpected revelation, but he spoke quietly enough. "Gareth Penderby? No, Meg. God helping us, it won't be like that this time. They won't dare go to those lengths. But that poor child is in their hands, and they will not be gentle. Please help us." He knelt beside her and laid an appealing hand on her wrist.

Without conscious thought he had used Ransome's name for her. Meg. It brought a puzzled look into her eyes, and for a moment she stared at him as though he were a stranger. Then she brushed one hand wearily across her brow and said, "I wasn't really sure before. But they were both gone all night that time. He said they'd been trapped in the passage by the tide; that it was only the smuggling, and if I told anyone I'd get the whole village into trouble.

But next morning — " Her voice died away and she shivered, and hugged her arms around her shaking body. "I can't bear it." And then, abruptly, "What do you want to know? I'll tell you anything I can."

At the back of his mind Charles was aware that she had already told them a good deal. But it must wait. The rescue of Nell was of more urgent importance.

"This passage that you speak of. Where does it lead? Could they have taken her there? Or is there any other place that you think we should search first?"

She eyed him doubtfully. "There's only the passage," she said at last, slowly, "and the old ruined house that stands above it. Crow's Nest, they call it. There's a way up to the house from the shore. I don't know of any other place where they might have taken her."

Charles had sprung up eagerly, and was striding about the kitchen. "I know the place you mean," he said. "On the coast, just beyond Winchelsea. God! I had thought it tumbled into the sea long ago. If they have indeed taken her there, then I know what to do. Indeed — " he laughed, a strange hard sound that held nothing of merriment — "I doubt I know the place a good deal better than either Sir Nicholas or Master Rudd."

He continued his leashed-panther pacing, and presently began to jerk out instructions to Giles. "I want a rope. Thirty feet of it, thin and strong. A good sharp axe — a dozen cleats — iron ones would be best, but I'll make do with wood at a pinch. Timing's important too."

The restless prowling stopped. One foot absently hooked up a stool to the kitchen table, and he sat, elbows on the scrubbed deal, chin on his clenched hands, thinking aloud.

"Full tide at — say — eight o'clock. No time to do anything before then. Nor will they expect it. But as soon as it falls far enough, let's say by midnight, they'll be looking for me. No doubt they've left some helpful clue to make sure I find the place. Now if I were Sir Nicholas, I'd wait in the living-room. A man lifting that trap is completely vulnerable. Yes. That's what they'll do. And they'll expect me as soon as the entrance is clear. So — we go beforehand and surprised them.

I'll ride Marquis — he's fit and fresh. You get over to Springbourne, Giles. You can ride Marshall — plenty in him still — acquaint Jasie with the situation and our plans, and muster what gear you can. And bring back Galoon. I may need your help with the first escalade."

The voice was crisp, incisive. His eyes were bright and keen, with a look that Giles knew well. Only the prospect of imminent and preferably hazardous action so stirred him. Uninvited, Giles too drew up a stool and sat facing his master.

"Be a little plainer, Sir, if you please," he drawled in his broadest Sussex, which had the desired effect of making Charles grin as he glanced up impatiently. "How do you propose to 'go beforehand and surprise them' if the water's in the gallery? You're no merman, as I do know of, and there's no other way into that place."

Charles's grin widened wickedly. "Oh yes there is. Shame on you Giles! After all the years you've rubbed shoulders with the Regiment! What do cleats and a rope suggest, cloth-head?"

Giles accepted the insult with an

amiable twinkle. "An escalade, Sir, like you said, though myself I'd rather choose a good sound ladder. But just what you're proposing to climb has me foxed. If it's Crow's Nest, you'll be wasting your time. The only windows that aren't blocked up are the ones in the living-room, and like you said, they'll be expecting you there. And a man climbing through a window is just as badly placed as one coming through a trap door."

"Hardly, Giles, hardly," returned his mentor critically, "but I'll allow it's not a good attacking position. You must do better than that. Think again."

"You could knock out one of the loopholes easy enough," decided Giles, "but they'd not accept a stripling. Besides, you'd be heard. So what — " he broke off, his eyes widening in indignant, half humorous surprise. "Now why didn't I think of that?"

"Perhaps because you never scrambled all over the place when you were a youngster, as I did. The whole of one summer that place was my castle — my frigate — my pirate island. I know every stone. My only doubt is whether the

294

chimney which gave such easy access to a ten-year-old urchin will give me such smooth passage now."

They got down to working out the details. Giles thought there would be no difficulty in getting the necessary equipment from Jasie, but was puzzled that pistols were not included.

Charles hesitated. "Perhaps I should carry a pistol. I don't somehow see it as a shooting affray. All I want is to bring Nell off safely, and if possible to avoid a scandal that would cause her a great deal of distress. The other affair must wait. It would seem that Miss Smithson may well be able to help us there, at least in the matter of Gareth Penderby's death."

"All the same, Sir, I'll feel a lot easier if you're armed."

Charles nodded. "Perhaps you're right. Though it means I shall be cumbered about like the knights of old, for the rope and the cleats I must have, and the axe is likely to be more use than the pistol."

"Not so much between the two of us," said Giles cheerfully. "You'd better carry the pistol, and I'll take care of the rest."

"Now what can have given you the notion that you were coming with me?" wondered Charles pensively. "I know I said I might need your help on the first escalade, but once that is safely accomplished you will keep well clear of the whole affair. No" — as Giles broke into expostulation — "that's an order. Perfectly sound, too, from the military point of view," he added in soothing tones, as Giles looked distinctly mutinous. "You are my line of communication and my reserves. So far, what is happening inside Crow's Nest, even if it is indeed the place we are seeking, is all surmise. If both of us go in, our whole strength is committed. I may need you to mount a rescue operation. Also I reckon they won't murder me unless they can make sure of you too, so we are safer apart. Now" — ignoring Giles's continued mutter of protest — "what do I wear for this foray? The devil's in it that I was never taught the proper rig for chimney climbing. What do you suggest?"

"That you let me do it," exploded Giles once more.

Charles, already under considerable strain from natural anxiety, lost patience. "Damn it, man — look at yourself," he snapped. "Are you the build to go sliding down chimneys? I may even stick myself." Then, relenting at the sight of Giles's crestfallen countenance, "And if I do, I'm relying on you to come and haul me out. Besides, this is a private matter between myself and Sir Nicholas. It's no part of my military duty. And your duty is perfectly plain — to mount a patrol on the outskirts of Crow's Nest, so that you can report to my cousin at Trevannions if anything goes amiss. It's a pity we haven't got him here. I'll go bail for it he's a good man in a crisis, and he's a much better figure for the job than either of us. But we're wasting time. Off you go to Jasie, while I finish my preparations here."

Obediently Giles went out of the kitchen, and then, on a sudden inspiration, put his head round the door to say, "Why don't you enquire whether our friend Ransome left his leather waistcoat behind? Seems to me it would be just the thing — what the best chimney sweeps are wearing," and with this final sally he retired in good order.

In the multitude of plans and conjecture that had crowded through his mind, Charles had forgotten the drooping silent creature crouched on the stool in front of the hearth, even to the extent of discussing her disclosures with Giles. But at the mention of Ransome in Giles's parting words she stirred to life, lifting a face of pathetic appeal to him as she faltered out, "Sir — do you know where he is? My Tom?"

Charles's heart was touched to pity. The poor woman had been far more sinned against than sinning, and she had done her best to put things right. Furthermore he had Emma's word for it that she had tried to protect Nell. Perhaps above all he was moved by sympathy with her desperate anxiety over someone dear and precious whose present state and whereabouts were unknown.

"Why, yes," he said reassuringly. "He is at Trevannions — my home, you know. He had a fall yesterday, and sustained injuries to his head and arm, but they are not serious and he is being well looked after."

The look of relief, almost of bliss, on her face, caused him a few guilty qualms over this very much expurgated version of the truth, but what else could he have told the poor soul? Nell would have to take him in hand, he decided, over this business of telling the truth. Nell. Where was she now? And in what case? There was no one to tell *him* soothing half truths about her well-being. His only relief was in action.

"Could you make me a meal of some kind? Anything will do, but I haven't eaten since morning and we may be out all night. And I think Giles's idea was a good one. Will you look in Ransome's room and see if you can find that waistcoat? I am sure he will not grudge me the loan of it." And as she bustled away, lightfooted and eager to serve him in her release from the fear that had haunted her all day, he took the stairs three at a stride, first to check the priming of his pistol, then to indite certain letters to be given to Giles for safe keeping should any accident befall him.

19

THE pride that had sustained Nell during the scene with her uncle and the innkeeper deserted her abruptly once her prison door was closed and she had heard the bar thumped into position. Helplessly she looked around for some shelf or stool on which to set the lanthorn. There was none to be seen, and at last, fearful lest her shaking hands should drop the precious burden, she put it down on the floor.

She leaned against the wall, a trapped, trembling little creature, her terrified gaze seeking to penetrate the gloom of her surroundings. Gradually the shaking of her limbs subsided and her eyes became accustomed to the darkness. The lanthorn threw a small circle of light on the dusty boards, but here and there were other threads of light, light which must come from outside, blessed daylight.

There were only a few inches of candle left in the lanthorn, but if she extinguished it with a view to saving it for a time of greater need, she had no means of rekindling it, and nothing, nothing, would persuade her to call her jailers to do so. It might be Rudd who answered the call. Best to use the light while it lasted to make a careful inspection of her prison.

The task did not take long. The threads of light, she discovered, came from crevices in the rubble that blocked the windows, but her small hands could make no impression on the rough stones when she tried to pull them out, and when she had persisted till her fingers were sore, she gave it up. At one end of the room was a wide stone hearth, still powdered with the ash of the logs that had once burned upon it. Standing within it she could see, far above her head, a square of sky, but the chimney opening was far above her reach, and there was no box or stool on which she could climb. Escape did not lie that way.

There was nothing in the room that offered either help or comfort. A few dead sticks and scraps of dried moss from a fallen bird's nest lay scattered on the hearth. Perhaps, when the candle was almost done, she could gather them together and kindle a tiny blaze to hold back the terrors of the dark for a few more moments. She turned once more to the seaward wall and the blocked loopholes — and was granted a spark of hope. The last one, the one nearest the fireplace, was only shuttered. Under ordinary circumstances the fastening would have been beyond her strength, for the boards were warped with the damp so that they were jammed tightly against the rusted iron bar that locked them into place. She wrestled with the corroded metal in a fury of desperation, her hands torn and bleeding, until she succeeded in forcing one end of the bar out of its bracket. It yielded at last with a vicious spring caused by the pressure of the shutter, and the end caught her cheek, inflicting a deep ugly scratch. She did not even notice it. With the utmost caution she eased out the other end of the bar and lowered it softly to the floor with one hand, holding the shutter pressed into position with the other. She was consumed by terror that some sound might betray her activities to the men in the room below. Then they would come and stop her — perhaps tie her hands, so that she would be completely helpless. A little sob, half fear, half fury, escaped her, as she struggled to lower the heavy oak shutter to the floor without a sound.

Then it was done, and light poured in to illuminate a portion of her prison. But after the first moment of triumph her heart sank. No more than the chimney did the window offer any hope of escape. It was built in two sections, separated by a solid stone pillar. Each part of the aperture was perhaps six inches wide and about three feet high. She could look out. She could thrust out an arm. But even for her slenderness there was no possibility of squeezing through, and to smash the stone pillar was quite beyond her, even if she attacked it with the shutter bar, while in any case the resultant noise would inevitably bring her jailers to investigate.

Bitterly disappointed, she leaned her cheek against the stone bar and stared out at the deserted seascape. Away to her right the setting sun was turning the sky to golden glory. A solitary kestrel was hovering against the glow. She watched it drearily, envying its freedom to come and go at will. If only it could carry a message to Charles. With the thought, hope and courage revived. Giles must have missed her by now, and he and Charles would already be seeking her. She must be ready when they came. And at least, now, she could signal if anyone came near enough. Also, came the next thought, she could perhaps tie something to the stone bar to indicate where she was held.

Her handkerchief was too small, and a search through her ridicule produced nothing suitable, but it did disclose the tiny scissors that she usually carried. As quickly as possible, for the light would soon be fading and a signal would be no use in the dark, she cut away the ruffled flounce that trimmed the hem of her dress and then wrenched at the gathering threads until they broke, so that she had a long strip of fabric to tie, streamer fashion, to her prison window. The little breeze that always came with the rising tide caught it and fluttered it gaily which cheered her a little, though she wished that she had chosen to wear white, or at least some other colour than green which would have shown up better. Eagerly she scanned the distant slopes to either side, but could detect no sign of life. As a final measure she tied her handkerchief to the end of the green streamer. Then there was nothing more that she could do except watch and wait.

It was already growing cool in the barn-like room, but not for worlds would she replace the shutter. She shivered a little and wondered how long she had been imprisoned, and what her uncle meant to do with her. There had been a grimly frightening note in the remark he had made about her bestowal. In the failing light, chilled and faint with hunger, many things seemed possible that she would have laughed to scorn in normal conditions. She was, she found, by far too familiar with the various classic legends of wicked uncles in old romances. She tried hard to fix her thoughts on Charles and the imminence of rescue, but found herself instead wondering whether it was really possible for her uncle to have her shut up in a lunatic asylum, as had happened to the heroine of one particularly lurid novel. Her growing hunger made it appear much more likely that he intended her to starve to death. She wondered when he would bring her food, and water, too, for she was very thirsty, then recollected that it would probably be Rudd who came to wait on her, and decided that she would rather endure the pangs of hunger and thirst than endure the man's foul presence. It was perhaps fortunate that she had not heard her uncle promptly negative Rudd's suggestion that he should carry some of the food that he had brought to the prisoner. "By morning," Sir Nicholas had added, "she'll be so devilish sharp-set, she'll not stop to wonder whether the food's drugged or not."

Kneeling on the floor beside her open window, Nell stared into the darkening sky. Already the first pale star was pricking out. Beside her on the dirty floor the candle flame guttered in a pool of tallow, but her spirits had sunk so low that she made no attempt to kindle the few twigs on the hearth. At least, she thought, gazing thankfully at the calm heavens, she was not condemned to total darkness. Last night — was it really only last night? — the storm had quite obscured the light of the moon, but tonight there was scarce a cloud, and she could at least rely on that faint illumination. Once again she tried to estimate how long she had been shut in this room. It sounded as though the tide was in, but as the little bay lay in the shadow of the bluff she could not be sure. Till the daylight was quite gone she had strained her eyes for signs of rescue. Now, hungry, cold and frightened, she kept her listening vigil under the moon, until the dark head drooped sideways against the rough stone sill, and, worn out by her exertions and her fears, she slept.

In the room below, secure in the knowledge that the rising tide had filled the gallery, her captors relaxed their watch and made such dispositions for their comfort during the next few hours as the miserable amenties of the place allowed.

Still deeply unconscious, Jim Cooke lay oblivious of the miseries of cramped limbs and insidious cold that awaited his awakening.

A darker patch of shadow that resolved itself into a small boat rounded the headland and crept quietly into the bay.

* * *

It was an odd little scratching tapping noise that awakened her. She tried to spring up, but subsided into a small heap on the floor as chilled and stiffened limbs refused to obey her will. Realisation of her miserable situation flooded in upon her at once.

She fixed her scared gaze on the door, fearful lest she should see a widening line of light appear, but nothing happened. The sound of her own breathing seemed unnaturally loud, but not loud enough to muffle a gentle pattering noise which seemed to emanate from the fireplace. Rats? Oh! Surely there could not be rats in this bare attic. What could there be for them to eat? She licked her dry lips and peered about her nervously in the gloom, then struggled to her feet and groped about her for the shutter bar. Thus armed, she retreated into the corner by the window, prepared to hit out at anything that squeaked or scuttered.

Out of the darkness a hollow voice whispered, "Nell?"

She must be dreaming. There was no one in the room with her. Yet surely — She held her breath, listening intently.

"Nell!" came the eerie whisper again, louder this time, and followed almost at once by the same pattering noises that had so startled her before. But a rat couldn't speak. Hardly daring to believe that her ears were not playing tricks, she crept out of her corner into the patch of moonlight. "Yes," she whispered back. "I'm here. Where are you?"

He was beside her as she spoke, strong arms gathering her up completely and holding her close, and she clung to him with all her strength. Relief at finding her apparently unharmed held him dumb for a moment, and if one or two tiny sobs escaped from the overwrought girl in his arms, such a weakness was very understandable. Almost at the same moment they both dragged themselves back to a semblance of normality, the girl blushing furiously in the darkness as she realised the shocking impropriety of her behaviour, and releasing her frantic clutch, Charles considerably assisted in a rapid re-orientation by the discovery that along with an armful of clinging feminity he was clutching a remarkably unyielding iron bar.

He set her gently on her feet, still keeping one steadying arm around her shoulders, while with his free hand he removed the intrusive bar from her grasp and laid it quietly on the floor.

"Have they hurt you?" came the urgent anxious whisper again.

She shook her head. "No. I'm all right." Then, with a sudden access of joyous realisation, "Quite all right, now that you've come. But I was so frightened. I thought you were a rat, and I was going to hit you with that," and she nudged the shutter bar with her toe, and suddenly giggled. "I s-seem to make a p-practice of hitting you over the head, don't I?" she whispered, half-way between tears and laughter.

Charles hoped she wasn't going to succumb to a fit of hysterics, though goodness knew she had cause enough. "A most reprehensible habit," he replied gravely. "Perhaps it is fortunate that I rarely choose to enter the house by a window, and never by the chimney, so perhaps we shall not come into collision too often."

Nell quite missed the pleasant implication in this remark, having seized instead on its offered information. "The chimney! Of course! It was too high up for me to reach without something to climb on, but I did *look*," she urged, anxious that he should not find her inadequate as a comrade in adventure.

Apparently he did not. "Did you? Well done, little soldier," he said gently. "I, on the other hand, found it a remarkably tight fit, and twice at least I thought I was stuck for good. I began to have visions of Giles lighting a fire below to force me out, as I'm told they sometimes do to the poor brats who sweep our chimneys. And I very much fear that Ransome's waistcoat will never again be the same handsome garment that it was," he went on, divesting himself of it, shaking it free of soot and dust, and putting it round Nell's shoulders. "But it certainly saved me from one or two scratches, and now it will serve to warm you, for you're as cold as a little stray frog."

The waistcoat still held the warmth of his body. Nell folded the scuffed leather close and hugged it to her, with a queer but delightful sensation of a warmth that penetrated to her very heart.

Charles meanwhile was unwinding a coil of rope which had been bound around his body under the waistcoat. "'Twas this pesky thing that nearly brought me to point non plus," he explained. "I dare not drop it down, lest it should fall down the other flue and be lost to us."

Nell was puzzled, not understanding that a flue from one of the downstairs rooms opened into this one, but there was no time to pursue the matter just now. There were more important matters that she wanted to know.

"How did you discover where I was," she asked curiously, "and which room I was in?"

"Why, Miss Smithson directed us to this place, God bless her, and once we saw your signal it was all quite simple.

You did well to think of that, my girl," he commended.

Nell was quite glad of the darkness which hid her blushes at this precious praise. "Where were you then? When you saw my signal?"

He perked a head laconically over his shoulder, busy in checking that the pistol had not suffered in his rough descent. "Back there. On that little hillock."

"But I looked and looked until it grew too dark, and I never saw you."

Charles chuckled. "My colonel would have had me courtmartialled if you had," he grinned. "You forget I'm a soldier, and a Light Bob at that. They don't exactly encourage us to go exposing ourselves on the sky line. I saw your signal, and I even saw you tie your handkerchief on it. After that we were able to lay our plans quite accurately. Now — " he had laid pistol and axe on the window ledge and the coil of rope on the floor below it, together with the shutter bar — "you and I are going to see if those plans will work."

"Are we going up the chimney?" enquired the lady with deep interest.

He shook his head "No. I couldn't expect a lady to make so undignified an exit." It seemed unnecessary to tell her that the council of three — for Jasie had returned to the Fleece with Giles — had unanimously agreed that no female, however plucky, would manage the difficult traverse of the slippery roof and the dangerous descent over the loose surface of the chasm. "You are going out through the window in the best romantic tradition, though I cannot, alas, promise a waiting post chaise and four — unless they be sea horses. You'll have to make do with Jasie and a boat. He's below your window now, though you can't see him." He leaned close to the embrasure and whistled a few notes of Lilliburlero, and from far below the softly completed phrase drifted back to them.

Charles smiled contentedly. "I take it your captors are snugly established in the parlour below, waiting for the poor simple fly to walk into the trap. How many of them, do you know? Was Cooke in league with them?"

Nell uttered a little cry of distress. "Oh poor Jim! I had quite forgotten him. No — he cannot have been an accomplice, else why should Rudd have struck him down? He said he was bringing me to meet you, and I am persuaded he really believed it."

If this were so, it seemed to Charles unlikely that Jim was still alive. In any case Nell's safety was his first concern. Jim, poor innocent blunderer, would have to wait.

"So there's just the pair of them? Sir Nicolas and Rudd?"

"Yes. But Charles — I can never get out of that window. I did hope so myself when first I found that I could open the shutter, but it's much too narrow. And if we try to break out the stone bar they'll be bound to hear us and come up."

"Exactly so. Just what I want them to do. The trouble is that they may not both come. If by any chance they do" — there was a pregnant little pause — "then maybe you won't need to go out through the window after all. But what's more likely is that only one of them will come. They'll surely think one man's enough to deal with one small slip of a girl. You see," he teased, "they don't know your predilection for hitting your visitors over the head."

Nell was a little reassured by his easy confidence, but she couldn't help wishing that they were both safely on board Jasie's boat. Then she chided herself fiercely for cowardice. Here was adventure such as she had always dreamed of, and shared moreover with the man whom by now she was near to worshipping, and she was wishing herself safely out of it! She couldn't see how they were going to escape, she didn't want to see how Charles meant to deal with her abductors. Resolutely she folded together lips that showed a distressing tendency to tremble, and resolved to do just as she was bid without wasting time with what Papa would have described without hesitation as foolish female vapourings.

Charles had now produced a candle and tinder box from his breeches pocket, and having lit the candle perceived the discarded lanthorn, which he seized upon with an exclamation of satisfaction. He then proceeded to make a careful inspection of the stonework of the embrasure, finally giving the lanthorn to Nell to hold while he grasped the stone pillar with both hands and wrenched at it with all his strength. Nell watched anxiously. The stone budged not a hairsbreadth. He met her anxious gaze with a cheerful grin, visible even in the moonlight. "Solid as bedrock," he declared. " 'Twill take my weight, let alone yours," and he knotted one end of the coiled rope round the pillar, testing each knot with care. Next he hauled in Nell's signal streamer, and having detached the handkerchief and returned it to her, proceeded to wind the strip of cloth round the thin rope where it crossed the edge of the sill.

These preparations completed, he lifted the coiled rope on to the ledge, and turning to the watching girl picked her up bodily and seated her on the improvised cushion, so that her face was on a level with his.

"Now," he said, and she could sense the mounting tension in his voice and in the nervous grip of his hands on her waist. "We're going into action, you and I. All the stonework at this side of the loophole" — he laid a hand on it — "is loose and rotten. I'm going to force it out to make a passage for us. As soon as I begin they will hear us, and someone will come. I shall have perhaps a minute to work, then I must stop and make ready to receive visitors. Your part, then, is to take this bar and make as much noise as you can, banging on the stonework. Don't worry about trying to loosen it — I'll do that later — but just make sure that whoever comes up comes right into the room to stop you. Is it understood?"

She nodded solemnly.

"Here's my pistol then. It's loaded but not cocked. Don't fire unless you must. I'd like to bring the pair of us off without having to make a lot of explanations afterwards." He smiled down into her trustful eyes, picked her up, and held her for a moment in a brief hug. "Here's good luck to us both, my girl," he said softly against her hair, and without further ado set her down in her sheltered corner, out of the way of fragments of flying stone, and applied himself with axe and crowbar to the crumbling stone work.

20

RUDD busied himself with adding the final touches to his preparations, his mind happily occupied in the contemplation of lifelong blackmail. Dangerous it could be of course, but with one of Sir Nicholas's kidney, a man who wouldn't soil his lily white fingers with the touch of violence, an enticing prospect. Those bundles of hay from the barn where Sir Nicholas's bay had found a temporary stable had been a good idea. They would start a fine blaze. The straw mattress on which that gentleman lay stretched, shielded from its contamination by his cloak, could be added to the conflagration at the last moment.

On an empty keg beside the hearth stood the remains of the food he had brought at Sir Nicholas's behest. He, with his niffy-naffy ways, had not approved the coarse fare, chewing his way disdainfully through a slice of cold pie, and nibbling at the cheese like a nun at a lemon. All the more for those who appreciated good plain tack, thought Rudd, biting into a generous wedge of pie and smearing away the jelly that dripped down his chin with the back of his hand. He slopped some brandy into the dirty chipped cup from which Sir Nicholas had sipped with such obvious revulsion. Yet it was good brandy, he decided, rolling it round in his mouth before gulping it down and taking another bite of pie.

"A few hours' sleep," he mimicked aloud, "is all I need. I must keep my mind clear, so that I may approach the new day's problems alert and fresh."

"Bah!" He spat as close as he dared to the sleeping man. But for his part, he wouldn't fancy taking those 'catchits' as Sir Nicholas called them. He had watched curiously as the gentleman had tilted back his head, poured the powder on his tongue, then swilled it down with a mouthful of brandy.

"Yes," Sir Nicholas had said, upon his interested enquiry, these were the same catchits that would do for Missy. He had condescendingly spelled out the word, since to Rudd it was unfamiliar, and had further explained that while one would give you two or three hours of sound sleep, three would produce a deep unconsciousness. A larger dose — Sir Nicholas shrugged. Then he had settled himself down on his unsavoury bed, leaving him, Rudd, to do all the work, and within minutes had fallen deeply asleep.

At least he had been abstemious with the brandy. Rudd, lifting the bottle, one of the last run, to the candle flame, saw that it was still half full, and contentedly poured another cupful. That was the way of it, he decided philosophically. Some had catchits and a mattress. Others had an old blanket and a sup of good brandy, and so thinking he tossed off the draught with a celerity that would have startled even the members of the Hellfire Club. Sir Nicholas had selfishly sprawled himself in the middle of the mattress, but maybe a hard-working innkeeper could use the odd corner as a pillow. Rolling himself in the coarse blanket he lay down on the floor and settled himself as comfortably as the circumstances permitted.

He was not allowed to sleep for long. It seemed as though he had scarcely closed his eyes when an ear-shattering racket began overhead. He sat up, cursing, and looked instinctively to his bedfellow for instructions. Sir Nicholas slept on as peacefully as though the noise were some sweet lullaby. Rudd scrambled to his feet, pulling off the enveloping blanket which had tangled itself about his legs. There was no time to be wasted. That hellish din would be audible half a mile away, and though in general the place was utterly deserted at this hour of night, one never knew when some damned nosey tide watcher might take it into his head to prowl around the purlieus of a house which rumour freely connected with smuggling.

He started for the stair, and then, on a sudden afterthought, turned back and picked up Sir Nicholas's riding whip. Missy should be given a good sharp lesson, and if Sir Nicholas didn't like it, he should stay awake and keep his niece in better order. Lips curled in a smile of pleasurable anticipation, he lumbered up the steep stairway and lifted the securing bar away from the doorway, yelling out to the girl as he did so that she'd better stop kicking up that row, or he'd come in and make her. A particularly loud crash drowned the end of his threat, followed almost at once by a perfect fusilade of blows. He grinned contentedly, imagining the terrified creature within battering frantically and uselessly at the unyielding stone, left the bar lying against the wall, and pulled the door open. Just as he had expected, the girl was hammering frantically at the window frame. He noticed with some surprise that she had even managed to prise one or two of the stones out of their setting. But as he made towards her, she dropped the bar, and, to his amazement, picked up a very serviceable looking pistol. Where the devil had she found that? He didn't suppose she'd have the pluck to fire it, even supposing it was loaded, but it looked uncommon nasty. He hesitated for a moment, and in that moment a pair of powerful arms encircled him in a close if unloving embrace, and a deep voice said gently in his ear, "Ah! My helpful friend, Mr. Rudd, hirer of paid assassins. Try doing your own work, Mr. Rudd, and see if you have any better luck than Tom Ransome."

The heavy crash of falling stones, followed by the sustained clamour of Nell's pounding on the window frame, had at last penetrated to Sir Nicholas's drug-bemused brain. He sat up slowly, his eyes dazed and stupid. His sleep had been too brief to permit the effect of the drug to wear off, and it required a considerable effort of will to bring his surroundings and the events that were taking place into focus. Pandemonium had broken loose overhead. The floor shook to the stamping of heavy feet, and to the thump and roll of struggling bodies. From his position on the hearth he could see that the bar was down and the loft door open, but even if Rudd had decided to rape the girl while he slept, no female could ever put up the sort of fight that was raging over his head. He could only assume that the hour must be far more advanced than he had thought, and that Rudd must have fallen asleep — probably in a drunken stupor, the sot, in spite of his strict orders to stay awake and watchful — and so had permitted Trevannion or his groom or both to steal a march on them. Though how they had managed to negotiate the passage, raise the trap and reach the girl without arousing either himself or Rudd, was a mystery that at the moment he could not solve.

With careful concentration he got to his feet and approached the open door, whence the sound of battle emerged with unabated fury. Cautiously he mounted, step by step, until he was able to obtain a clear view of the combatants, just in time to see Trevannion break from Rudd's hold and land a couple of heavy body blows before retiring out of distance and circling for another opening. Behind the contestants, clearly illuminated in the moonlight, stood his niece, a pistol in her hand, her whole alert poise clearly indicative of a fierce determination to use it if necessary.

Under the stimulus of this shocking scene, Sir Nicholas's bemused brain cleared with surprising celerity. The two men were in the middle of the room, and as he cautiously raised his head another inch Rudd plunged at his antagonist in a wild attempt to land a crippling blow. Neither man had any attention to spare for what was happening at the door, and the girl, at the far end of the room, would not dare to fire for fear of hitting her lover, even if she saw what he was about.

Quick as a flash Sir Nicholas was up the remaining stairs, had closed the door and heaved the bar into position. Whatever the outcome of the fight, all three were now safely caged. Slightly breathless, he leaned against the door and considered what he should do next. He could, of course, simply retire from the scene and disappear gracefully, but that would mean the abandoning of all his ambitions, and with the flow of French gold cut off it would not be long before his mounting debts caught up with him. Were there any means by which he could still salvage security out of apparent catastrophe?

He came slowly down the stairs, deep in thought, oblivious of the noise overhead, and his glance lighted upon

Rudd's carefully built pyres. Of course. A moment's consideration convinced him that the scheme contained no flaw. And a smile of the purest amusement curved his mouth as he thought of the painstaking care with which Rudd had created the instrument of his own destruction. With the exception of Trevannion's groom, all the obstacles to his success were trapped in a room which would shortly be a raging holocaust, and the groom, whatever his suspicions, could prove nothing. There was not a shred of evidence to connect Sir Nicholas Easton with the mysterious tragedy that would shortly be enacted. He could even take time to add his revolting bed to the bonfire. He stooped and dragged it to the foot of the staircase.

Rudd had been only half right when he said that the luck was with them, for now, without any effort on his part, he would dispose of Rudd along with the rest. For him alone the gods of chance had smiled. With meticulous care lest he drop hot tallow on his well-kept apparel, he took the candle from the lanthorn and moved from one pile to the next, lighting each in several places to make sure that they were well ablaze. Through his activities he gradually became aware that the sounds of conflict in the room above had ceased. He even found himself wondering with mild interest who had won. He hoped it was Trevannion. It was a pity that he would never know.

He picked up his cloak and shook it, carefully picking off one or two straws that clung persistently, and put it about his shoulders. His whip seemed to have disappeared, but he had better not stay to look for it, since already the room was full of smoke. He stooped to the trap, and as he raised it an axe crashed against the timbers of the attic door. Sir Nicholas smiled. The door was two inches thick, of weathered oak and hard as iron. The axe would be blunted long before its fibres yielded.

He lifted the trap door clear of the cellar entrance. The draught from below would help his fires to burn more fiercely. Already the attic stairway was ablaze. Carefully he descended the cellar steps to the gallery entrance. There he stopped. For a long moment he stood aghast. Then his fingers moved with quiet purpose to the pocket that held the cachets.

The luck had run out at last. In the belief that Trevannion had made his entrance by way of the gallery, he had miscalculated the state of the tide. Water was lapping gently over the lower rises.

21

HE had not planned to do more than mill the man down — knock him out perhaps, as he had done Ransome — and so clear the way to freedom for himself and Nell. Yet looking down at that hideous mask of agony and death, at the betraying purple marks across the throat where his fingers had choked the life away, he felt neither guilt nor shame. It was not even because in his heart he felt that he had only exacted just payment for the death of Gareth Penderby. Standing in the shadows beside the door, he had seen the evil lust on the man's face as he had come in, the purposeful grasp on the whip which was intended to subjugate his proud slim girl. That whip had signed the man's death warrant. It had roused Charles to an uncontrollable fury which would endure all punishment so that it was finally assuaged by killing. The punishment had been considerable. Rudd had been a powerful opponent, not unskilled in wrestling and boxing, and master of many a cunning trick that might easily have defeated Charles's greater science, had he not been sustained and inspired by the raging passion within him.

He dragged himself to his feet, and turned rather blindly to the corner where Nell waited.

"I'm sorry, child," he said, hoarsely, heavily, "you shouldn't have been subjected to that exhibition. But at the end, it was him or me."

"Is he dead?" she said wonderingly. And when he nodded, her voice came fierce and quick. "Then I'm glad. He was a beast and a brute, and he deserved to die."

Charles stared at her. He had expected tears — vapours — even reproaches. It seemed that women were not the delicate sensitive creatures that he had been led to believe. Certainly this one wasn't. She was looking up at him anxiously, and one hand came up tentatively to touch his bruised and battered face. "Has he hurt you dreadfully?" she asked with childlike simplicity, and then, on a penitent gulp — "It's all my fault. If only I'd done as you said, none of this would have happened. I'm truly sorry."

Painful though the action was, Charles had to smile. There was a good deal to be said for a philosophy which could accept abduction, violence and murder itself, and reduce the whole situation to nursery status as something that could be expiated by an expression of frank penitence.

"Are you *sure* you're all right?" said the anxious voice again. "He hasn't injured you seriously?"

"No." Though not for want of trying, he thought, remembering one or two of his late opponent's less endearing tricks. "I'm quite all right. I think perhaps we might try the door now, since there is only your ingenious uncle to oppose us." He picked up the axe, testing its edge against his thumb, and summoning up his depleted energies for the next task, but Nell had turned away from him and was standing, head up, sniffing the air as he had seen hounds do when taken at fault.

"Do you smell smoke?" she said sharply. "Something burning?"

He stopped. A couple of blows on the tough oak had already suggested that more than one tired man with an axe was required. Obediently, he too sniffed. There was no mistaking it.

"The window it must be, after all," he said cheerfully. "Dear Uncle Nicholas has set the place alight beneath us."

The task was not nearly so difficult as he had feared. Quite a light tap from the axe was sufficient to set the perished mortar showering down in clouds of dust, and though he would have preferred a stouter crowbar, a man must be thankful, and the shutter bar, though rather too flexible, proved adequate to the work. One by one the larger stones were dislodged, as the smoke, seeping up between the floorboards, thickened in the room.

It really did not take too long to make an aperture wide enough to permit the passage of Nell's slim person.

"There," he said thankfully, putting down his tools. "Now for Jasie and his boat." He put his head out of the window and whistled again, a joyous bubble of impudent sound. And prompt to cue, back came the response from below.

"Good man, Jasie," he murmured softly, and then to Nell, "It would seem that your father trained his colour serjeant almost as well as he trained his daughter. You won't be afraid, I know. You can trust Jasie and me to take care of you. I'm going to bind this end of the rope in a loop round you, and lower you down to the boat. It won't be very comfortable, I'm afraid, and you may come down wide of the boat, but there's no need for silence now, so if you find I'm lowering you straight into the arms of Father Neptune, just yell, and I'll stop. The boat must be within a yard or two, and Jasie will be with you within seconds."

Nell heard him to the end, and then shook her head firmly. For one dreadful moment he thought she was frightened of the descent. Some people, he knew, couldn't bear heights. Then she said, quite coolly, "That opening's not big enough for you. I noticed your shoulders wouldn't go through, only your head.

I'm not going down until you've made it bigger. Then I'll know you can follow me as soon as I'm safely down, and we'll both be all right."

Her lips were stubbornly set. Unless he picked her up bodily and dropped her over the ledge, she wouldn't go, and since such rough and ready methods would add considerably to the risks of the descent, he dare not use them. There was no time to waste in further disputation. He picked up the bar and set to work on the next stone.

"I thought you were going to do as you were told in future," he grunted, as he flung his weight against it.

Nell didn't answer. Having gained her point she was quite willing to let him have the last word. Meekly she busied herself with a demure, almost housewifely air, in placing the axe and the pistol conveniently to hand on the windowsill. There was her handkerchief, fallen on the floor, and she bent to pick it up. It was not her handkerchief at all, but a packet of papers. It must have fallen out of Charles's pocket. She glanced up at him, but he was wholly absorbed in getting the greatest possible leverage on his frail crowbar, so she stuffed it into her ridicule, thinking to give it back to him later, and hung the frivolous little bag on her arm. Then she was ready — and another large stone fell away from the wall.

"That should do it." And to prove it, he thrust head and shoulders through the gap he had created.

There was no further protest from the lady. She stood submissively under his hands as he dexterously knotted the rope around her waist and instructed her how to grip it once she was clear of the sill.

"Even so, I fear it will cut sorely," he finished. "But it is not for long. And if you can keep your hands just so" — he showed her — "they will protect your face. I'll lower you as steadily as I can, but there's always the danger of bumping against the wall. There" — he tested the knots — "are you ready? Up with you then."

He lifted her to the opening, bidding her kneel on the ledge facing him, and took two or three turns of the rope round his forearm. She felt him grip the rope girdle about her waist and lift her clear of the sill, so that her feet were dangling in space, and she tried not to think of the drop below, fixing her eyes on his intent face.

"Try if you can feel the wall with your feet," he said quietly. She stretched out one foot obediently. The wall was comfortingly close. There was even a tiny projection that offered a toe-hold.

"Just try to imagine that you are walking down the wall," said the calm voice, as though they had all the time in the world at their disposal, and his grip shifted along the rope until at last she hung suspended from it, leaning a little outward, her feet pressed against the wall.

"Good girl. Now, take hold of the rope as I showed you, and away you go. Don't look down," came the final injunction, and she felt herself being lowered steadily and slowly.

It was not so frightening as she had thought, though she found it impossible to keep her feet on the wall, and once or twice was jarred against it as she swung helplessly, like a spider on a thread, she thought inconsequently. Then friendly hands reached up from the darkness and caught her ankles, guiding them down till her feet touch the thwarts, and Jasie's comfortable familiar voice was telling her to let herself flop down in the boat, or she'd have it over, like as not.

"Oh Jasie!" she gasped, suddenly close to tears, and clutching at his arm. Never had she dreamed that his gruff Sussex voice could sound so sweet in her ears.

"Nay, lass, give over, do. Sit thee still and let me come at they knots. 'Tis time Sir Charles was out of it, for it's getting too warm for comfort." His fingers tugged and fumbled at the knots which had naturally tightened under Nell's weight. She turned her head to glance over her shoulder at the house above her, and gave a startled exclamation of horror. Flames were already leaping from one window of the living-room, and the others were lit by the lurid glow from the inferno that raged within.

"Oh *do* be quick," she begged in agony, for surely by now the very floorboards must be alight and Charles in deadly danger. Why, oh! why had he let her down in such leisurely fashion, when he must have realised — Her own hands flew up frantically to wrestle with the intransigent knots, only to be smartly slapped away by Jasie's horny palm.

"*Will* you hold still," he growled, and perforce she subsided, though the task seemed to take him an interminable time.

"There's no need to fret yourself to flinders," he said more kindly. "This end's not caught yet. 'Twill be just the smoke and heat. And we'll soon have him out of it now," as the last obstinate knot yielded and the rope fell away from her.

There was no lack of light now. Jasie cupped a hand to his mouth and yelled, "All clear below," at the top of his powerful voice, but even so it seemed that it might not penetrate the roar and hiss of the flames. However, the slack rope was in itself message enough. He picked up the oars and backed off a little, so that he could see when Charles climbed out of the window and began his descent.

He slid down fairly swiftly when at

last he came, setting the rope swinging wildly, so that his landing was not near so neat as Nell's had been, one foot hitting the gunwale, which set the boat rocking and Jasie to cursing with vigour and enthusiasm until the newly arrived passenger managed to steady himself and roll into the bottom of the boat.

He picked himself up and shoved aside some spare gear to make a place for himself on one of the seats. "All aboard, Captain," he announced cheerfully if a trifle breathlessly. "I hope that is the correct nautical expression. And now, if you please, we'll make all plain sail for the other side of the bay. I expect Giles has chewed his fingers down to the knuckle by now."

Jasie, correctly interpreting these instructions to mean that he was at liberty to proceed, shipped his oars and pulled slowly away. "Tide's just about on the turn," he said reflectively. "Time it's up again, there'll be nothing left of Crow's Nest."

As though to point his remark a section of the kitchen wall slowly collapsed outward and cascaded into the sea, and tiny flames spiralled gaily skywards around the naked timbers that had supported the roof.

It was an awesome sight, and the three in the boat watched in silence, broken at last by Jasie, who said in blunt matter-of-fact tones, "And a hem good riddance too. It's been naught but a den of thieves and murderers these ten years past. You're lucky to come out of it alive, Miss Nell, and that's God's truth."

Nell acquiesced gravely, and then, suddenly, gave a sharp cry of horror. "Jim!" she said, to Charles's startled enquiry. "Jim Cooke. Perhaps he's still in there."

A moment's rapid explanation was sufficient to acquaint Jasie with the facts. He shook his head dubiously. "If he's in the room at the far end there's just a chance. Anywhere else there's none. Try it if you think fit, but I can't lay the boat alongside, not with the tide falling. You'll have to swim for it."

Charles stooped to pull off the rough country brogues that he had borrowed for his climbing. Then he took the pistol out of his belt and laid it on the thwart, while

Jasie took the boat as close as he dared to the one bit of Crow's Nest that was not yet ablaze.

In the event, very little swimming was necessary, for which Charles, by now beginning to feel rather more than weary, was duly grateful. A dozen powerful strokes, and he was stumbling over the rocks which came up to the wall of the house, with a foot or so of water purling about his ankles. To smash away the boarding that covered the window frame was simple enough, but his first attempt at entry was repelled by the choking smoke. Hastily he hauled off his wet shirt. Holding this improvised mask over his mouth and nose, it proved possible to effect an entry, and he had not taken three steps in the smoke-filled gloom before he tripped headlong over something which proved on closer investigation to be the body of a man. It was gagged and bound. It was still alive. It could only be Jim Cooke.

Fingers and brain having reached this conclusion, it remained only to haul the poor devil out of his present uncomfortable, not to say dangerous situation. This was not quite so easy as it sounded. The shirt, bound into position by its sleeves, hastily knotted, kept slipping down, and it was quite impossible to work without it, and he found himself lamentably feeble when it came to heaving the dead weight over the window sill. But somehow it was done, and with a final effort he half-dragged half-carried his burden to the water's edge.

There was a sizeable patch of shingle by now, and surely the fire could not touch them here. The boat was gone. Jasie, with characteristic good sense, having watched his protracted struggle at the windowsill, had crossed the bay to bring up the reserves. Soon he would be back with Giles. For the moment — blessedly — no further effort was required of him. Quietly, comfortably, with a facility developed over years of campaigning, Charles dropped his head on the unconscious man's shoulder, and slept.

22

SHE sat up in her own bed at the Lamb and stretched out a hand for the cup of chocolate that Bella had just set down. It must be late, for sunshine flooded the room as the maid drew back the curtains. In this familiar comfort the dramatic events of yesterday seemed like a bad dream, but her own bandaged hands were evidence enough of their reality.

Bella twitched the folds of the curtains into prim symmetry and turned back towards the bed, obviously eager to linger and gossip. When Nell asked where everyone was this morning, the intelligent hand-maid wasted no time on reporting the whereabouts of irrelevant personages. "Sir Charles was here early," she announced, "but he wouldn't let us wake you. He had to ride over to Trevannions, he said, but would do himself the honour of calling upon you this afternoon." She savoured the well-conned phrases with satisfaction and delight and relapsed comfortably into her natural style.

"Eh, Miss, such a set-out as never was," she began eagerly. "Master was over Winchelsea way this morning, and they do say as Crow's Nest be burnt right out. Only the walls left standing. And two dead men they found," she went on with ghoulish enjoyment. "To think, if it hadn't been for Sir Charles, Jim might have been burned to death! Wonderful brave it was, to go in after him with the place ablaze like that. Jim says he'll never be able to thank him, specially after what 'e'd done. And then Mistress Woodstead sent me off after some of her cordial, so I didn't rightly hear what that was. Jim's still abed too, and mistress won't let me next nor nigh him," she ended a little resentfully, and then, bobbing her head shyly, explained that she and Jim were thinking of keeping company reg'lar like.

Nell expressed sympathetic interest in this budding romance and heard all about Jim having no family of his own, which had made Bella, one of the blacksmith's large brood, feel 'heart sorry for him,' and these interesting confidences might have gone on indefinitely, had not Jasie been heard shouting for Bella, and enquiring where the dratted wench had got to this time. She fled, leaving Nell to finish her rapidly cooling chocolate in peace, and then to stretch herself luxuriously, revelling in the sensation of complete security as much as in the benison of the warm sunlight that was pouring over her. Her limbs were still stiff and sore, and she was surprised to discover a number of bruises that she had not even been aware of receiving. Her hands had suffered the most, but Emma had bathed them tenderly and bound them up with her own elderflower salve. There had been a scratch on her cheek, too, she remembered, and scrambled out of bed to patter across to the mirror to inspect it. She was so engaged, tentatively fingering the long purple weal, half bruise half scratch, and hoping it would not leave a scar, when there was a gentle tap on the door and Emma came quietly into the room.

"So you've decided to wake up, have

you, slugabed? And high time too," she said with her habitual calm. "Now let that scratch alone, and it'll heal just as it should. I came to help you dress, seeing as you'll be awkward with your hands bandaged."

She moved about the room, quietly and without fuss, pouring water into the basin, finding fresh underwear and stockings, and helping her nurseling with tapes and buttons that were difficult for bandaged fingers.

"I'll send Bella up to unpack for you presently," she said, as she was engaged in brushing out the silky dark hair, with caustic comment on its tangled state. "Jasie brought all your things over from the Fleece this morning, so you've no need to set foot in *that* place again. Dr. Hilsborough said you were to keep your bed today, but I knew you'd not be for doing that, so I've had a couch set in the garden, and you can rest there, where I can keep my eye on you."

Nell met her glance in the glass and wrinkled her nose in a naughty little gesture of defiance, which swiftly changed to a rueful grimace as the scratch on her cheek made itself felt.

"Yes," nodded Emma grimly. "You'll do just as you're told for once. A fine pickle you got yourself into, and all through going your own way from what I can make out. No. Sir Charles didn't give you away. 'Twas Giles told me you'd disobeyed orders. Why, I thought 'twas some ragamuffin had strayed into my kitchen, with your dress all torn and soaking wet and your hair in this state."

Nell composed her features into an expression of meek penitence, but inwardly her heart was singing. It was such bliss to hear Emma scolding in her own inimitable way. And this afternoon Charles was coming to see her.

Resolutely she shut her mind to this joyous thought. Even Emma's kindly presence was an intrusion on the privacy in which it should be savoured. She asked instead how Jasie did after his share in last night's adventure, and whether Jim Cooke was mending. Emma's reports were satisfactory. She, too, had many questions to ask. The child had been in no case for talk last night. She had

348

sat quietly, as though half dazed, during the painful business of having her cuts and scratches cleansed. "Yes," she had said, she was very hungry. So Emma had brought her a bowl of bread and milk. And what was there about that to upset anyone? Yet she had scarcely lifted the spoon to her lips before it had splashed back into the bowl, and down went her head on her arms in such a storm of weeping as had quite dismayed Emma, so that she had been obliged to ask the doctor to mix a composing draught for Miss Nell when he had finished with Jim Cooke.

Whatever he had put in it had certainly had a beneficial effect, decided Emma rather grudgingly, for she set little store by doctor's medicines, preferring rather to rely on the salves and simples that she brewed herself. She brought out her elder-flower salve now, and having helped her charge into an enchantingly pretty dress of primrose jaconet with green riband trimming, unwound the bandages from the torn and battered little hands and proceeded to annoint them with the soothing balm.

It was pleasant to be installed on the couch beside the sun-dial, with a sunshade to protect her from the glare and Bella to run backward and forward to make sure she had all she needed, though not so pleasant to be restricted to the couch. Riding or driving, she accepted, would be out of the question till her hands mended, but Emma would not even let her stroll about the garden. Because of the bandages she could not sew, and even turning the pages of a book was surprisingly difficult. The hours which must pass until she could expect to see Charles seemed interminable. She lay watching the bees working busily over a bed of thyme, her eyes half closed, and stared in indignant disbelief when Emma roused her to say that she had slept long enough, and now she must take some nourishment. It seemed impossible that she could have slept the morning away, and she was much inclined to blame Dr. Hilsborough's potion, but once awake she realised that she was hungry, and Emma's chicken broth was delicious, with tiny tips of asparagus hiding in its velvety depths, while the raspberries and cream that followed would have tempted a sybarite — or a maiden in love. Certainly she was so far restored as to be able to give a rational account of her unpleasant experiences. Emma busied herself with some sewing, listened, asked an occasional question, and finally wanted to know how she had managed to get herself as wet as if she had fallen into the sea. "For that good green cambric is ruined, all stained with sea water as it is, let alone the ruffle cut off the hem, and it just new come from Miss Pemble's hands."

This innocent question seemed to touch a sensitive spot, for Nell blushed furiously and then confessed that she had indeed jumped into the water.

"But only just at the very edge," she offered in extenuation. "It was when we had brought Giles over to help lift Jim into the boat. I could see them both lying there, and I was so dreadfully afraid that he was dead. The boat was going so slowly and I just had to find out, though it made Jasie dreadfully cross. And after all he was only asleep."

Strangely enough Emma seemed to find

this tangled and inconsequent account with its oddly unrelated pronouns, both comprehensible and satisfactory, and merely said that it was a pity that she hadn't chosen one of her older gowns to go stravaiging about the seashore. Nell accepted the mild rebuke meekly, thankful to be spared further enquiry, and at last summoned up courage to ask the question that had troubled her mind since Bella's disclosures of the morning.

"Sir Nicholas — has anything been seen of him?"

Emma nodded gravely. She had been prepared for this. "He is dead. Though just how he came to die is something of a mystery, for Sir Charles says it must have been he who set the place on fire. Jasie thinks that he must have misjudged the state of the tide and reckoned on escaping by way of the passage, for it was there that the men found him when they searched the place this morning."

The news was only what Nell had been expecting. If two bodies had been found, as Bella had reported, then the second was most likely to have been that of her uncle. She had feared and disliked him, and knew that in firing Crow's Nest he had sought to encompass her death. It was a strange and rather solemn thought that in so doing he had brought about his own. Her thoughts turned for a moment to the unknown aunt in London and to the small son of whom Sir Nicholas had spoken once or twice. She pitied them sincerely. And she remembered the one occasion when she had been truly grateful to him.

"At least he took my part against that horrible Rudd," she said.

The church clock chimed two, and Emma folded up her work, declaring that she must be off to tend her son. He had, she said, been remarkably patient, seeing that though small he was male. "Knows just what he wants and clamours to have it at once," she said indulgently. "They are all so." With which dark hint she retired into the house.

Quite soon Nell heard the sound she was waiting for, and made pretence of shaking her head over the manner of it, for the horses were being driven at a break-neck speed, quite unsuitable to the heat of early afternoon. She heard them pulled up, clattering and sidling over the cobblestones, and Jasie's deep voice raised in greeting; heard, too, the note of surprise in his voice, though she could not hear what was said. There was the sound of laughter on the air, so she was content to wait till he came to her.

But when at last he came, she rose slowly to her feet in amazement not unmixed with anxiety, for he had come to her in all the glory of full regimentals — dear, familiar buff facings, gleaming silver lace, and above them the proud dark head, the lean brown face of the man she loved.

Startled, even a little awed, by this formal magnificence, she looked up at him almost timidly. Then his hands came out to her, and he said eagerly, softly, "Nell, my darling," and swept her into his arms without more ado.

Doubt and timidity were swept away in that rapturous embrace. With Charles's kisses warm on her lips, Nell knew herself equal to anything. Whatever he demanded she would give, even — oh! desolation itself — if he ordained that she must stay at home in safety at

Trevannions while he went back to Spain, she would obey. And this was her immediate fear, for surely he would not have presented himself in uniform if he had not been recalled?

Even as she steeled herself to accept whatever news he brought, he relaxed his hold slightly, one arm still about her shoulders, the other hand gently pushing up her chin, so that her eyes met his.

"You will marry me? No more pretence, but a true promise?"

She nodded solemnly, for suddenly her throat felt choked so that she could not speak.

"Shall we be married at once then? If you will consent, I shall charge my new cousin to procure a special licence when he goes back to town. Then you shall come with me when I rejoin the regiment," he tempted.

"Oh! Yes, please!" breathed Nell, too overwhelmed by such a blissful prospect to be concerned about a proper maidenly reticence.

Charles laughed, and bestowed a brief hug on her. "Emma was quite right," he pronounced. "There's the makings of a first rate general in Emma."

Nell looked at him in puzzled enquiry.

"You see," he explained, drawing her down to the couch and seating himself beside her, "I consulted her this morning about the propriety of making my declaration so soon. Instinct prompted me to toss you over my saddle bow and make off with you, yet we have been acquainted barely two weeks, and I feared that you might later regret such a rash proceeding. Emma, bless her, counselled me to go ahead and chance my luck, assuring me that you were just meant to be a soldier's wife, which of course I already knew, and adding, for good measure, that she personally had selected me as being good husband material. Indeed," he added with a twinkle, "it seems that you and I have had very little to do with the affair. Emma had planned it all, and we needed only to conform to her wishes."

Nell nestled up to him contentedly, putting up one hand to finger the scarlet cloth of his coat. "I was afraid, when I saw you dressed so, that you had already been recalled," she confessed.

He looked half amused, half rueful. "Emma again," he admitted. "All Emma. You must understand that by this time we were on famous terms. She was so good as to advise me as to the best method of conducting my courtship. 'Take her by surprise,' she said, and strongly recommended the wearing of my best uniform. It seems she has, not unnaturally, a touching faith in the charms of a red coat, and thinks that no reasonable female could resist a lover so attired. And so indeed it proved," he pointed out, wickedly teasing.

"As though I should care for such a thing," declared Nell indignantly. "You know very well that I loved you just as much last night, when you wore no coat at all — and indeed no shirt either."

He lifted a bandaged hand in his, and since no other part of it was available pressed his kiss on the slim wrist. "Yes, my love, I do indeed know. I was not perhaps so deep asleep as I seemed." His eyes quizzed her unmercifully, and her colour flared.

"Oh!" she gasped. "Infamous!" and tried very hard to look severe, frowning darkly at him and primming up her lips, but the bubbling happiness within her would not be repressed, and the soft mouth trembled into laughter as she excused herself by explaining, "I was afraid you were dead."

Then of course he must catch her in his arms again and present her with certain tangible proofs that he was very much alive.

"We must go and tell Emma," she said presently, dreamily.

"Yes, indeed. Though if you had heard her scolding me last night after she had put you to bed, you would never dare hope for her approval." He grinned. "'Rapscallion,' and 'blackavised pirate' were among her more polite terms. And what she had to say about tearing up my good shirt and going about half naked reminded me strongly of my own old nurse. And all the while she scolded she was tending my various bruises and scratches and sending poor Jasie hobbling about for hot water and salve and sticking plaster, and then for his best shirt to put on me so that I should be decent."

Nell breathed a tiny contented sigh. It

was good to hear him speak with such understanding and appreciation of her dear Emma. "It is always her way," she acknowledged. "She must truly value you, to scold so. You should have heard her rating me, for spoiling my dress with sea water." For a moment she looked back at last night's events, and suddenly remembered the papers she had picked up during those last tense moments in the attic at Crow's Nest.

"I wonder what Emma did with my ridicule," she said. "I hope your papers weren't anything important, because I'm afraid it got pretty wet."

"What papers?" asked Charles idly.

She explained, but Charles vowed that the papers were none of his. "For I emptied everything out of my pockets to make room for those wretched cleats."

"I wonder where it came from then? It certainly wasn't there before you came. Why! It must have been hidden in the wall. Oh! Charles! Suppose it is a pirate map, and will show us where treasure lies hid? He was once a pirate you know, the old man who built the house."

Charles was deep in love. Though an

observant eye might have seen his lips twitch, he neither laughed at the fantastic suggestion nor raised any objection when his love insisted that they must find the missing ridicule immediately.

Emma, having welcomed Sir Charles with a proper formality that relegated both last night's scolding and this morning's conniving to a distant past, was pleased to offer her respectful felicitations to the happy pair, and then added that should Sir Charles wish to put off his good uniform, he would find all his belongings laid out in his own room.

Pressed about the ridicule, she said that it was quite spoiled, but that she had put the contents to dry out in the side oven. Not that there was much — just a pair of scissors, a handkerchief, a packet of papers and a buckle from a slipper, which she would sew on again, if only Miss Nell would remember to give her the slipper.

Nell had not waited for the end of this speech but had run eagerly to look in the oven, and now pulled out the mysterious package. It was at once obvious that this was no ancient map or document, for the outer wrapping, though stained and dirty, was a sheet of perfectly modern writing paper. When this was removed, several closely written sheets remained, and though in places the ink had run, yet much of the writing was still clearly legible. Charles watched with warm amusement as an eager child unfolded the limp sheets, studying them with an expression of growing puzzlement.

"I don't understand," she said after a moment. "It seems to be some kind of a list. There are numbers and dates, and look — here it says something about the 95th. See — the 95th will move to — Charles!" Her face whitened as realisation began to dawn on her, and at the same moment Charles leaned forward and without apology twitched the papers out of her grasp. A glance was enough. Not only were the details on which his eye fell perfectly comprehensible to him, but he also recognised the writing. It was the gracefully formed caligraphy of the gentleman who called himself Sir John Blackadder.

23

"THANK you, Miss Easton," said Mr. Christopher Pollett, accepting his cup of tea from an inexperienced hand. "Yes, indeed, that is just as I like it. You must permit me to tell you what a pleasure it has been to make your acquaintance, and how much I regret the necessity for my imminent departure. Yet no — how can I wholly regret it, since by going I may be of service to you and to my Cousin Charles? Shall we say that the selfish part of me regrets it? I take comfort in the thought that it will not be long before we meet once more — upon the auspicious occasion of your marriage."

Shyly Nell expressed her gratitude for these polite sentiments.

She found Charles's cousin a trifle overwhelming in his role as a languid sprig of an effete aristocracy. It was difficult to realise that this slim, fair, drawling young man was the same person as the first-rate horseman she had seen riding the rebel Marmion when Charles had brought her over to Trevannions earlier in the day.

Charles had been anxious to acquaint his cousin with their discovery without loss of time. Almost before she knew what was happening Nell found herself installed in the carriage, a bandbox containing her prettiest evening dress, hastily packed by Emma, on the seat beside her, and Charles promising that he would see that she ate a good dinner and would bring her back at a respectable hour, but that the news was so important that his cousin must hear it forthwith. She savoured the experience joyfully. Life would be like this now, she supposed — bustle and excitement and sudden hurried journeys. Her spirit leapt joyfully to meet it, and she had waved her good-bye to Emma with her face in such a glow of happiness as caused that loving soul to nod contentedly to Jasie and say, "She'll do now. It's just the life she was meant for, and Master Charles'll guard her well."

They had stopped briefly at the Fleece,

where an interested and delighted Giles had heard their news, and a very cursory inspection of Sir Nicholas's effects had produced specimens of his handwriting that would doubtless be of considerable interest to Mr. Gressingham and his colleagues. Taken in conjunction with 'Sir John Blackadder's' note and the newly recovered documents, they seemed to Charles to offer reasonably solid proof that Sir Nicholas was the traitor he had been seeking, and that Rudd had been acting in collusion with him.

They had not hurried unduly on the journey, for Nell was anxious to hear all that had happened in regard to Ransome, and how her disappearance had been discovered and her rescue planned. And once they reached the gates of Trevannions, the greys were allowed to slacken their pace to a walk, for now she was seeing the place with new eyes, since so soon it would be her home. As he had told her, it was not a mansion. There was no extensive park, the drive that led to the house running through rich pastures, where occasional clumps of trees provided a pleasant shade for the horses that were everywhere.

A horseman cantered gaily towards them, lifting a whip in salute — Cousin Christopher on Marmion, to whom he had capitulated whole-heartedly vowing that never before had he crossed an animal so perfect in conformation, speed and stamina.

"And manners?" Charles had asked, grinning.

But the devotee would have none of this base insinuation. Marmion, he declared, had just sufficient temperament to make him an interesting ride. It was some little time before Charles was able to check his rhapsodies sufficiently to present him to Nell, and then to disclose that they had discovered important documents which he trusted would supply proof of their suspicions. At this intimation just the faintest flicker of intelligence had crossed Mr. Pollett's well-bred but slightly vacuous countenance. He declared himself all eagerness to hear their story, but first, of course, he must see Marmion well rubbed down and safely bestowed, and then he must put off his own dirt, after which he would be wholly at their service.

Throughout the interchange he had controlled the dancing restless creature with an easy grace that gave no hint of the strength behind it. Charles had acknowledged a horsemanship far superior to his own, and Nell had felt that she could learn to like this new cousin very well.

While the housekeeper escorted Nell to a guest chamber, Charles had strolled round to the stables to oversee the attention given to the greys. Nell had tidied herself as best she could with her clumsy fingers, and then made her way down to the library, where Charles was impatiently awaiting the arrival of his cousin, and meanwhile perusing once more the incriminating papers. He sprang up to greet Nell with suitable marks of his esteem, and then, still holding her in his arms, burst out in a mixture of indignation and irresistible amusement, "Who do you think I found in the stables, very much at home, and actually instructing my farrier in the proper management of brood mares? None other than my friend Ransome!

It seems that after Cousin Kit had failed to extract any more information from him, they had somehow fallen into heated argument about the best conformation for a steeplechaser, and nothing would do but that Kit must forthwith hale my prisoner down to the stables to illustrate his theories by putting Marmion through his paces. By the time that they had spent a couple of hours looking over the young stock, Kit was so carried away by Ransome's knowledge and instinctive ability that he has offered him employment. It appears that he intends to set up a racing stable and vows that Ransome's talents will be invaluable. When I suggested that there were certain objections to the employment of escaped convicts, he said that could easily be dealt with. He would engage himself to get the fellow a free pardon — on account of services rendered in the present enterprise! When you consider the nature of his services, you will not wonder that I saw no cause for a reward!"

Though she shared his indignation, Nell could not but laugh. In her present mood of utter content, even Ransome was a figure of comedy. "After all," she pointed out, "he certainly had the worst of the encounter, and he seems to have been most unjustly treated in the past. I could not feel happy in handing him over to justice. So perhaps it is best that he should be found respectable employment, and then he may marry his Meg and they can be happy. For she has certainly deserved well of us, and I feel that we should make some provision for her future, since it is because of us, in a way, that she is now cast adrift."

Charles found the expression of serious philanthropy on her face quite enchanting, and must needs present her with another token of his regard, which to their mutual regret, was cut short by the entrance of Mr. Pollett.

Upon examination, that gentleman expressed himself as very well satisfied with their find. It seemed practically certain that the leakage of information, at least from this source, had been stopped, and that Gareth Penderby's death had been avenged. He would report the known facts to his superiors when he returned to town next day, taking with him the precious package of sea-stained papers. He also undertook the unpleasant task of acquainting Lady Easton with the news of her husband's death. It was unlikely, he thought, that there would be any public scandal over the affair. "We always keep this sort of thing as quiet as possible," he explained, "lest others should be tempted to follow a bad example."

They turned then, with relief, to more pleasant matters. Cousin Kit was all helpful acquiescence over the business of obtaining a special licence, and since Charles would certainly have to report at Horse Guards within a day or two, they could meet in town to settle final details for the ceremony.

"And you really don't desire a fashionable wedding?" Mr. Pollett murmured to Nell. "Admirable, quite admirable. My cousin is indeed in luck."

Nell scarcely knew how to answer this, so she asked instead how he proposed to secure a pardon for Ransome.

"Why, nothing could be simpler," he

said, widening his eyes innocently. "I have only to tell the truth."

Nell blinked. He grinned, the world weary man of fashion reverting for a moment to the mischievous schoolboy. "Well — perhaps not quite all of the truth," he elaborated. "I shall explain that he was engaged to murder Charles, but that as he came to know him better, so he came to regret most sincerely that he had ever listened to his wicked employers. That is quite true, you know. I'll swear he rued it bitterly by the time the pair of you had done with him. Eventually he was persuaded to reveal all that he knew. Yes — that's true as well, Miss Easton. The fact that he knew nothing to reveal need not concern the powers that be. Sir Charles was thus enabled to track the traitors to their lair," he concluded triumphantly.

Nell gazed at him, shocked but amused. Amusement triumphed and she gave her deep rich chuckle. But later, in the darkness of the carriage, a small hand curled itself confidingly into Charles's, and a shy voice enquired, "We shall never have to live in London, shall we?"

"Not unless you particularly wish it, my love," promptly answered Charles, who could think of nothing he would like less.

"I don't. Indeed I should dread it, for I am sure I should never know how to go on among a set of people who can present the truth so that it makes you believe something quite different."

Charles turned towards her and gathered her close. "But you know very well just how you should go on to make me adore you more with every passing moment," he whispered softly against her cheek, "and that is so very much more important."

THE END

THE WILDERNESS WALK
Sheila Bishop

Stifling unpleasant memories of a misbegotten romance in Cleave with Lord Francis Aubrey, Lavinia goes on holiday there with her sister. The two women are thrust into a romantic intrigue involving none other than Lord Francis.

THE RELUCTANT GUEST
Rosalind Brett

Ann Calvert went to spend a month on a South African farm with Theo Borland and his sister. They both proved to be different from her first idea of them, and there was Storr Peterson — the most disturbing man she had ever met.

ONE ENCHANTED SUMMER
Anne Tedlock Brooks

A tale of mystery and romance and a girl who found both during one enchanted summer.

CLOUD OVER MALVERTON
Nancy Buckingham

Dulcie soon realises that something is seriously wrong at Malverton, and when violence strikes she is horrified to find herself under suspicion of murder.

AFTER THOUGHTS
Max Bygraves

The Cockney entertainer tells stories of his East End childhood, of his RAF days, and his post-war showbusiness successes and friendships with fellow comedians.

MOONLIGHT AND MARCH ROSES
D. Y. Cameron

Lynn's search to trace a missing girl takes her to Spain, where she meets Clive Hendon. While untangling the situation, she untangles her emotions and decides on her own future.

NURSE ALICE IN LOVE
Theresa Charles

Accepting the post of nurse to little Fernie Sherrod, Alice Everton could not guess at the romance, suspense and danger which lay ahead at the Sherrod's isolated estate.

POIROT INVESTIGATES
Agatha Christie

Two things bind these eleven stories together — the brilliance and uncanny skill of the diminutive Belgian detective, and the stupidity of his Watson-like partner, Captain Hastings.

LET LOOSE THE TIGERS
Josephine Cox

Queenie promised to find the long-lost son of the frail, elderly murderess, Hannah Jason. But her enquiries threatened to unlock the cage where crucial secrets had long been held captive.

THE TWILIGHT MAN
Frank Gruber

Jim Rand lives alone in the California desert awaiting death. Into his hermit existence comes a teenage girl who blows both his past and his brief future wide open.

DOG IN THE DARK
Gerald Hammond

Jim Cunningham breeds and trains gun dogs, and his antagonism towards the devotees of show spaniels earns him many enemies. So when one of them is found murdered, the police are on his doorstep within hours.

THE RED KNIGHT
Geoffrey Moxon

When he finds himself a pawn on the chessboard of international espionage with his family in constant danger, Guy Trent becomes embroiled in moves and countermoves which may mean life or death for Western scientists.